Tales from above, below and places in between. Copyright © 2020 by Glenn Lomas. All rights reserved. No part of this book may be used or reproduced in a manner whatsoever without written permission.
Editor – John Ross
Cover design – Jenny Groat
Back cover design and book layout- Paul Gibson
ISBN – 978-0-9732674-3-3 (e-book)
ISBN – 978-0-9732674-2-6 (paperback)

Dedication
For Pat and Heidi Del-Gatto

Other works by Glenn Lomas

- The Challenge

Tales from above, below and places in between

Truth and Consequence

This is a story about the devil and his name is Maurice.

◊

Live from the seven rings of Hell it's the Truth and Consequences game! And here is your host, Satan!

<Applause> from the studio audience.

"Thank you Derek for that lovely introduction. Welcome to Truth and Consequences. We have three guests who are waiting in a sound proof room. They don't know where they are, only that they are on a new game show."

<Laughter and applause>

"Let's not waste any time now, shall we? Our first contestant is a home maker, she is 57 years old and her name is Linda. Let's hear it for Linda."

<Applause>

A short plump woman emerged from behind the curtains. She had been invited to the show only two days earlier. A man called her house and asked if she would like to appear on a new game show. To prove they were serious they wired $10,000 into her account. She was flown in on a private jet and was staying at a beautiful hotel with complimentary services.

Linda had never heard of the show before, but what did she care? She was $10,000 richer with the chance of winning other prizes and was living like a queen at the hotel. She wasn't used to such luxuries. For Linda, staying at a fancy hotel usually meant an overnight at a *Motel 6*.

"Next we have Brian, a 42 year old electrician. Give it up for Brian."

<Applause>

Like Linda, Brian had been invited to the game show two days earlier. But unlike Linda, he wasn't offered money and he wasn't contacted by phone. His doorbell rang with a beautiful woman waiting behind it. She told him he was selected out of thousands to participate in a new game show. He quickly lost interest and started to shut the door when the woman's high heeled foot stopped the door from shutting. Brian was about to yell at her when she made him an offer, "I'll let you fuck me if you say yes."

Brian stood at the door stunned when she pushed the door open and stepped in. When the door closed behind her, she grabbed his crotch and whispered in his ear, "Fuck me hard, and fuck me now."

Brian had a lot of sexual experiences, but this was by far the most exciting. She went to the cherry stained console table next to the door, pushed aside his wedding photos and sat on the edge. The woman spread her legs and lifted her dress to reveal she wasn't wearing panties. Brian didn't have to be asked twice. He awkwardly and quickly pulled his pants down and shuffled over to her with his pants around his ankles.

He started thrusting and she pulled his hair back, growling, "Fuck me hard, you bastard!" Brain was not used to a woman talking to him like this and he started to pump harder, and she responded with hip thrusts of her own.

She grabbed his hand and put it around her throat and squeezed his fingers shut. He started choking her, and she started moaning louder. With her face turning red, she grabbed his other hand and made him slap her across the face. Brain was stunned; he didn't know what to do. She bucked him and drove her heels into his ass as a reminder to keep fucking hard. He slapped her across the face again and when he did she moaned deeper and shuddered.

Her face started to turn purple when he released his grip. She grabbed his hair and with animal eyes, said, "No!" Brian smiled and gripped tight on her throat and gave her a hard slap which stung his hand. She responded with a muttered moan and more thrusting. He wasn't sure if he'd choke her to death but he didn't care. When he came, it was if he was a teenager again. He couldn't remember an orgasm so hard and intense.

When he backed away, the woman hoped down from the table, put back his wedding photo and handed him an airline ticket. It never occurred to him that she didn't have it in her hand when she came into the house, and she didn't have a purse. With her free hand she wiped away the trickle of blood which was coming from the corner of her mouth.

"When you land, I'll make sure there are more *like minded* ladies such as myself to take care of you." She winked at him and walked out his door.

Now he stood at a podium with lights, TV cameras and an audience in front of him.

"Our final contestant is a Darryl, a 66 year old CEO. Please welcome Darryl."

<Applause>

Darryl walked out with a hesitant grin on his face. He didn't really know what was going on. He didn't like game shows, didn't watch them, and certainly didn't want to appear on one. The last thing he remembered was leaving for the day from his office. He was putting on his coat when his secretary, like she always did when he was leaving, was going over the following days itinerary.

"Tomorrow morning you have an 8:30 breakfast with Mr. Simmonds. At 10:45 you have an executive conference call, followed by lunch with Mr. Sanville at Jaquilline-Luicille's. Mr. Edwards from personnel is meeting you at 4pm. And don't forget tomorrow night you are on that game show."

"Game show? What are you talking about?" he asked confused.

"It's called Truth and Consequence. You'll do great sir." His secretary said when she ushered him out the door. In front of the studio lights he couldn't recall his meetings he was supposed to have earlier that day. And he didn't recall ever saying yes to this. What surprised him more was that he was still standing there. He was a powerful man, with billions of dollars and hundreds of millions squirreled away from the tax man.

He could buy and sell every person on the set and in the audience. He didn't want to be here. He was going to be a laughing stock at his company and with his associates. Yet, as much as he wanted to leave he stayed and gave a shy smile to the cameras.

"Now for those who have never seen our game, it is quite simple. We will try to discover a hidden truth from your lives, and if we cannot, we will pay you out in cash," said Maurice.

<Ohh's and awe's>

"But if we discover your hidden truth, then you must pay the consequence."

<Ohh's and applause>

Darryl wanted to walk off the set right away. He had enough of this; he didn't want to be on any stupid game show and he certainly didn't want someone revealing any hidden truths from his life. He was a private man, and he liked to keep it that way. But as much as he wanted to leave his feet remained where they were. He looked at the crew for some sort of help but they all had their eyes locked on the host.

"Let's play... Truth and Consequence!" said Maurice.

<Applause>

Maurice walked over to the first podium. "How are you doing today Linda?"

"I'm very excited to be here," Linda said with a big smile, looking towards the crowd obviously enjoying the attention.

"Great to hear! We love enthusiasm," Maurice replied with a smile. "Do you consider yourself a truthful person Linda?

"Yes, of course."

"Excellent. No white lies? Ever cheat on your taxes?" He looked over at Darryl. "Don't worry Darryl, we won't ask you that one," he said with a wink.

<Laughter>

Darryl tried to walk off again, he had enough, but he was frozen in place.

"Well, I'm sure I might have told the odd white lie," Linda confessed. "But, nothing I figure too big."

"Wonderful," said Maurice with delight. "Let's find out from the person who would know you best. You're husband Edward!"

<Applause>

Linda's smile slowly faded. She didn't know Eddie was going to be here. He never mentioned anything to her. Her mind was blurred and confused. When was the last time she had spoken to him? Her memory was a fog. When was the last time he had seen him? Hadn't Eddie passed away five years ago?"

The curtains opened and on a platform stood Eddie. Linda was very please he dressed up for the show, wearing a nice suit. Eddie didn't like wearing suits. He didn't like dressing up at all; he always wore jeans and t-shirts. But the suit fit him well, and made him look more dignified.

Didn't she bury him in that suit?

"How are you Edward?" Maurice said shaking hands with him.

"Call me Eddie please."

"Sure thing Eddie. I'm sure you know your wife really well, right?"

"Better than most I reckon."

<Laughter>

"Do you consider your wife to be an honest woman, Eddie?"

"Yes sir."

"Well then, let's bring out a surprise guest. Your daughter Debra!"

<Applause>

Another curtain opened and a behind it was a cage with what appeared to be a person inside of it. The girl, whose age was hard to tell from her condition, was just skin on bones. She was lying in her own waste with a couple of empty water bottles inside. She barely had the strength to wave her hand to the studio audience.

Linda stood wide eyed. It had been years since she had thought of Debra at least 20, because that was how long ago she had died.

"Welcome to the show Debra," Maurice said happily.

Debra could barely whisper a thank you.

"Maybe you can help us out here dad," Maurice said. "It seems Debra is having a tough time talking. Can you give us the truth to why she is in a cage?"

"Well, Debra was trouble ever since the day she was born. She'd never shut up, always crying and crying. We'd hold her, leave her alone, yell at her to shut up, nothing worked."

"*Kids*. Am I right?" Maurice said looking at the audience.

<Laughter>

"I reckon. Anyways, she was always a problem. When she grew a bit, she was always a handful at school. Getting in trouble, yelling at teachers and other kids. After a while we just kept her home. The school, at first, would ask about her, but after a while, they stopped calling us. I figure they were glad to get rid of her."

"But how did she end up in a cage Eddie?"

"Well, I was getting to that." Eddie stood still on the platform. He never used his hands to gesture, just stood in place talking in a monotone voice. "When she as about 10, she started to run away. By that point she was a wild child.

"We tried locking her in her room or the closet, but she always got out. Well, anyways, one day I was at the dump, dropping off some drywall I tore down. I was redoing our washroom. Well, anyways, when I was there I saw a cage. I reckon it must have belonged to some big animal or something, probably for a really big dog or somethin'. I pulled my truck up near it and I dragged it close and I barely managed to get the cage on.

"Well, anyways, when I got it home I washed it off, and it cleaned up fairly well."

"A nice fatherly thing to do." Maurice said with a smile.

<Laughter>

In the cage Debra was able to lift her head slightly off the floor and gave a little nod.

"I reckon. Well, anyways, we got some rope and slowly lowered the cage down the stairs into the basement. When Debra saw it she tried to run away, but Linda grabbed her and tossed her inside. Told her it was for her own good."

Brian and Darryl looked with horror at Linda. She stood motionless, blinking, trying to come to terms of seeing her dead husband and daughter again. This wasn't what she signed up for. She wanted to go back to her luxury hotel room.

"We fed her every day and kept a bucket in there for a toilet for her. But like I said, Debra was a problem child, and sometimes she would miss the bucket or not get up off the floor to use it. She would soil herself and the stink was something terrible, let me tell you."

"By the looks of that cage, she couldn't stand up fully."

"Well, I reckon you're right with that." Eddie looked over at the cage and gave a little shrug and continued his story. "After a while I stopped going downstairs. It smelled like a pig sty and half of the time Debra would just scream or cry. Linda would go down and toss a bottle of water in the cage with some food. I think after a while we just stopped going down too."

"Debra died?" asked Maurice.

"Yep," replied the father.

<Ohhs and ahhs>

"I think we forgot about her for a week or so. When we went down, she was curled up dead. 15 she was. I don't reckon there was one day in those 15 years she wasn't trouble.

"We wrapped her body up in an old sheet and I took her to the dump and buried her. Didn't take much, she wasn't barely 70 pounds dead."

"Thank you Eddie for that compelling story."

<Applause>

Maurice walked over to Debra's cage. From inside his coat pocket he pulled out a gun, pointed it to Debra's head and fired.

<Applause>

Stage hands moved the cage off to the side, leaving a puddle of blood and brains on the polished floor.

Maurice put the gun away and walked over to Linda.

"Don't worry about seeing her again Linda. Her real spirit has been in a better place since she died in your basement. Trust us, *you'll* never see *her* again."

<Laughter>

"So, Linda? The game is Truth and Consequences. Is Eddie telling the truth?"

Linda felt a lump of bile growing in her stomach. She couldn't help but stare at Debra's blood and brains left on the floor. "Linda?" Maurice asked waiting for an answer.

She looked back over to Eddie. "I need an answer Linda."

"No, he's lying! That son of a bitch is lying!" Linda started screaming. "You're dead you bastard! You died years ago!"

"Come now Linda, we only tell the truth on this show," and he slowly raised his hand and waved it in front of her face getting her attention away from her dead husband. "Is Eddie telling the truth?"

Tears started running down her check. "He's not lying."

"It's time for a consequence!" Maurice announced joyfully.

<Applause>

A stage hand rushed up to the platform Eddie was standing on. He put a noose around his neck and rushed off. Eddie just stood there, not trying to remove the rope. The front of the platform was removed exposing its structure. Then the trap door under Eddie's feet opened. He hung twitching, unable to die, experiencing every sensation of hanging to death without the death.

<Screams>

The three contestants looked over at the studio audience only to see a fire. One of the audience members was on fire; the skin on his face bubbled and turned black. He clawed at the fire at his face removing the charred black skin, exposing red raw skin only to have it blacken again by the searing flames. The lady beside him was smiling, seemingly unconcerned with the man burning beside her. The flames caught onto the sleeve of her blouse and she quickly became engulfed with flames. Her screams filled the studio yet no one around her attempted to help them. The fire slowly spread to the rows in front and behind them feeding on more audience members. The people on fire didn't drop and die from the flames but survived its intense heat with no sweet relief of death.

"Don't worry Linda," Maurice said looking over at Eddie who was still twitching. "He's been with us for a while this is a walk in the park for him."

Maurice moved over to his right. "Let's meet our next contestant Brian."

<Applause and screams>

"Hi there Brian, tell us a little bit about you."

"No. I, I just want... I just want to go home."

<Laughs and screams>

The blazing fire had spread to over half of the audience. Those who weren't on fire, seemed oblivious to what was going on around them, and those on fire, even beating at the flames and peeling off charred skin, still attempted to laugh with the rest of the audience.

Maurice tilted his head back and gave a hearty laugh. Brian was sure he heard animal screams mixed in with the laughter. Like Darryl, he tried to run away, but was frozen in place.

"As they say in the business Brian, the show must go on! Let's bring out a special guest, you *may* recognize. Bring her on out."

The curtain lifted and a young teenage girl was standing there alone. She brushed the hair out of her face and gave a small smile to Maurice as he approached her.

Brian stood confused. He looked at the girl, and had no idea who she was.

"Welcome to our show. Can you please introduce yourself?"

"Thank you," the girl said smiling towards the crowd that were still on fire trying to escape the flames. "My name is Samantha Curry."

Maurice turned back to Brian. "Do you recognize Samantha, Brian?" Brian stood there still confused. He tried to run, but couldn't move. He had no idea who this girl was, and he didn't want to know.

"No?" Maurice said answering for Brian. "Well let's give you a hint." When Maurice turned back to the girl she was covered in blood and naked. Her face was beaten and swollen. Her throat was slit, along with cuts along her breasts, arms and torso. Most of her body was bruised and swollen.

Brian had the urge to throw up. His bladder released when he recognized the girl.

<Laugher and screams >

By now the entire audience was in flames.

He tried to close his eyes and turn away, but just like his feet, they stayed locked onto the bloody girl. Tears ran down his eyes, and he wasn't able to hold back the vomit as he threw up all over the podium in front of him.

<Laughter and screams>

"Oh, it looks like he recognizes you Samantha," Maurice said smiling at the young girl. "Why don't you tell us how you met?"

She started to talk, but only blood and bubbles escaped her mouth. She wiped her mouth with her hand and gave a shy smile.

"Sorry, it can be a little difficult talking with this," gesturing towards her slit throat.

<Laughter and screams>

"I met Brian about 14 years ago. Actually, I met his wife first. I was walking towards my car; I borrowed it from my parents to go to work at a strip mall 20 minutes away from our house. While I was walking towards my car, a woman called me and asked for help. She was carrying a large cake box. She told me she just picked it up from the bakery that was near the store I worked in, and she couldn't reach the keys in her purse to open the van door.

"I didn't think anything of it. It was a large box and she had both hands underneath to carry it. So I came over and she allowed me to reach into her purse for the keys. She said she wanted to slide it into the back, so I unlocked the door and when the door opened I was struck on the head with something. That was the first time I met Brian." She said smiling his way.

"His wife dropped the box and scooped my legs into the van. The box was empty there was no cake."

Maurice turned to Brian and moved his finger back in forth in a naughty, naughty fashion.

"I woke up in Brian's basement with him raping me. And over the next week he raped and beat me. His wife would come down to feed me, and lead me to the washroom   I was tied up the entire time. I would cry and plead with her to let me go, and she would stroke my hair and tell me things would be fine, that I should trust her."

"Did you?"

"Actually I did. She was really nice to me, and she would wipe the blood off my face after he beat me. She told me, that Brian was crazy and she was afraid of him too. She promised that once he left the house for a couple of hours that she would let me go, and together we would go to the police station so he would never do this to anyone again.

"On the last day of my life I was awoken with a hard slap to the face. I thought I was about to be raped again, when I realized it was his wife that woke me up with that slap. I had no idea what was going on, why she would do that to me, and then I saw Brian behind her. I figured he put her up to it. But I could see in her eyes, that she liked it. I knew I was going to die when I saw the knife in her hand.

"I was tied down and he raped me while she used the knife all over me. She even cut off my nipples," as she gestured towards her chest. I could tell Brian loved it, and she was getting off on it too. She would cut me then kiss him and cheered him on while she watched me being raped. When he climaxed, she slit my throat."

She looked down at herself and over at Brian who could not look away.

"They dumped me into a river, and I was found three days later. I was his first victim. He raped 14 women after that, killing 5 of them with the help of his wife."

"Thanks for sharing Samantha!" Maurice said as he walked back to Brian. "Now Brian, the name of the game is Truth and Consequences. Was Samantha telling the truth?"

Brian could not stop crying. He just wanted to home, but he couldn't move. "Brian? I need an answer please."

"I'm... I'm so sorry!" Brian cried out to the young girl. "I won't do it again!"

Maurice laughed, "I'm sure you won't Brian. But it seems Samantha was telling the truth. So we have a little surprise... let's bring out the woman whom helped kill Samantha, your lovely wife Carrie!"

<Applause and screams>

His wife Carrie was escorted out by two stage hands. She was visibly scared and was trembling. "Carrie, thanks for coming. You know your husband Brian here, and I'm sure you remember Samantha over there."

Carrie looked over and saw the bloody girl smiling who gave her a friendly wave. She let out a scream and tried to run, but she could not break free of the stage hands.

"No leave her alone! Please!" Brian pleaded.

<Laughter and screams>

"I'm sorry Brian. Let's see the consequence!" said Maurice.

<Applause and screams>

Carrie stared at the host wondering what was about to happen. Maurice stood there with a small grin on his face a happy, trusting sort of grin. She looked past him and she saw Brian. He was screaming and his face was contorted in fear. It looked like he was trying to escape an invisible rope around him. He stood still, but also had the appearance of thrashing. He was crying and screaming at her, she didn't understand what he was saying. She looked to the stage hand to her left and she started to scream too.

The two stage hands had morphed into enormous demons. They had black eyes, with a forked tongue and rough, scaly skin. The claws at the end of their fingers dug deep into her arm, tearing the flesh and their forked tails slithering behind them lashing out slicing the back of her legs with their sharp edges. If you asked her before the show what a demon would look like, it would be this.

Brian saw two completely different demons holding his wife. If you asked him before the show what a demon would look like, it would be this. The beasts threw his wife down to the ground, tearing off her clothes and cutting into her flesh. They spread her legs and Brian saw the one demon's penis. It was so big, it looked outrageously fake. The one thing that didn't appear fake was the sharp ridges that worked its way from the base of its penis to the head of the monstrosity. Brian didn't have a chance to scream out a warning when the demon thrust itself inside of Carrie.

She screamed out in pain and blood flowed from her vagina. The other demon was tearing at Carrie with its sharp claws, tearing the flesh off her body. Her screams continued while Maurice continued with the show.

"Last but not least is Darryl. Are you enjoying yourself?"

Darryl could not look away from the demon rape that was happening in front of them. Linda's husband was still twitching from the end of a rope off to the side. Eddie had soiled himself and was trying to talk or scream but only a gurgling noise came out. Darryl didn't belong there, he just wanted to go home, and he whispered that thought, the volume lost in his throat.

<Laughter and screams>

"I'm sorry Darryl, we're not done the game," Maurice said getting closer to him and putting a hand on his shoulder. "Your story is a different one from Linda's and Brian's. You didn't starve your daughter to death and you didn't rape and kill young women." Over Maurice's shoulder Darryl could still see Carrie being raped. The other demon was now raping her while the other was tearing at her throat with his teeth. Carrie kept screaming, and there was so much blood. It was impossible for her to be alive, he thought, she should be dead. Then he looked over and saw Eddie, purple bloated face, eyes bulging, twitching on the Gallo's. He should have died long ago too.

"No Darryl you led a different life. You are a man of business, you are a man of wealth and power. You can say you worked your way from the ground up. You were 16 years old when you started working for VonBatten Industries sweeping floors. From there you worked your way to the mail room leading into answering phones before you were given a Jr. Sales Associate position.

"From there you thrived and caught the attention of management. You were promoted to Senior Sales Associate and became a Jr. Executive at the age of 35. The youngest in company history! After 7 years you became a Vice President which you held on for only two years when they named you President, the title you still hold today."

<Applause and screams>

"During your time as President of VonBatten, your company has grown immensely with the purchase of other companies and making an economic empire under the VonBatten flag. Subsidiary companies in mining, oil, pharmaceuticals, media outlets, bio technology and numerous other fields.

"You must be very proud of your achievements?"

"Leave me alone! Let me go, I didn't do anything wrong!"

"It sounds like it's time to play..."

<Truth and Consequence>

"You have five children and three wives correct?"

"Leave them alone you bastard," Darryl screamed out.

<Laughter and screams>

"Now, now. They're not here. They really don't want much to do with you anyways. Am I right?" Maurice didn't wait for an answer. "Your true family was business and making money."

"There is nothing wrong with that. I made a lot of people rich and gave them better lives. I might have failed as a husband and a father but that doesn't make me a bad person!"

"No," agreed Maurice. "There is nothing wrong with making money, but making money at what cost?" Maurice stepped away from the podium and walked past Carrie who was still being raped and torn apart by demons and Eddie who was still swinging and twitching.

"Let's introduce the VP for VonBatten Industries, Neal Grey!"

<Applause and screams>

The curtain opened for a short man wearing a tailor made suit, similar to Darryl's. Maurice stepped up to the man and put his arm around his shoulders, "Tell us the truth about Darryl."

The man shuddered when Maurice touched him. He looked at Darryl and started to talk.

"Darryl is a very smart business man, I looked up to him and he mentored me for years. He was almost like a father to me..."

"The truth Neal." Maurice interrupted.

"We have an oil rig off the coast of Somalia, ahh that's in Africa."

"Thank you Neal, we know where it is. But thank you for the geography lesson."

<Laughter, screams>

Neal looked at the audience who were still on fire, trying in vain to escape the flames. He shook his head as if he was dreaming and looked at the host who was giving him a polite smile. Maurice gestured with his hand to continue."

"Oh right. Sorry. Anyways on the rig we had a malfunction and we lost containment. We figured we were losing about 2,000 barrels a day spilling into the ocean. It was serious, but compared to something like the BP explosion in the Gulf of Mexico, it was just a minor event.

"During an emergency meeting our engineers said we could shut the rig down and do a full repair, or still maintain production with minimal shutdowns as they made repairs. Full shut down would last for 4 to 8 weeks with zero oil production. Partial shutdowns, the job would take 6-8 months with continued leaks but we'd still be able to operate. Darryl decided on the partial shutdowns."

"You son of a bitch!" Darryl yelled from behind the podium. "We had clean-up crews in position to isolate any oil. We followed protocol, and on the advice of expert engineers we chose an option where we could still be productive at the same time isolate any environmental risks!"

"Neal?" Maurice questioned.

"Environmental laws are very lax in third world nations. We put containment booms in place, but they were placed three days after we discovered the leak. Also we had rough weather and the booms could not contain with the waves we were experiencing. The oil reached land on the coast of Somalia and part of Kenya. We made payments to both governments and any legal actions were dismissed."

"We paid fines you bastard! You make is sound like a payoff. We paid for any clean-up costs!"

"Many parts of the shore line that had villages on its edge were not cleaned up. Much of the coast has what appear to be little balls of crude oil along it. The clean-up should have cost us hundreds of millions not to mention the economic damage done to local fishermen and their health."

"I don't belong here!" Darryl shouted again. "I don't belong here with these... these monsters!" he said jerking a thumb in the direction of Linda and Brian. "I'm a business man! People depend on me! If I don't do my job people lose out. People invest their children's education and their retirement in my ability to make tough decisions.

"I'm not perfect, but I worked within the laws that other people made. We paid fines to governments and it is their responsibility to do the proper things with the money we give them. The fact that you would have me here for a fucking oil spill is god damned ridiculous!

"Has my company affected the environment, sure, I guess. But no more or no less than any other industry. Yes I have fired people, and I have bought up companies and shut them down and sold its assets. I have also hired many people and given them a decent wage. I'm in the business of making money and I was very good at it. Hell, I was the best at it. But I also made a lot of other people rich, and we helped a lot of people. We gave a lot of money to charity and helped thousands. Yet, I didn't go looking for publicity for it. Don't judge me because of my success!"

"We also found the cure for cancer," Neal said in a monotone, almost nonchalant way.

"Neal! What the fuck are you doing?"

"What did you say Neal?" Maurice asked with an intrigued expression.

"I said we found the cure for cancer."

"Shut the fuck up Neal!" But Maurice turned to Darryl and put his finger to his lips in a shushing manner.

"We have a research department in our pharmaceutical company. We weren't looking into cancer research if truth be told. The team we had were looking at blood pressure medications. It was all a simple mistake really.

"One of the researchers was supposed to inject a healthy rabbit with a trial sample which hoped to stabilize a person who was experiencing a dangerous increase in blood pressure. We would test the formula on healthy rabbits to see if they had any side effects. Well, the person who went for the healthy rabbit, accidently took one from the wrong cage. It was a rabbit which had tumours on it. The formula we had was mistakenly made. This was well before the computerized control system we use today. Someone simply grabbed a wrong ingredient and added it in with the high blood pressure dosage. The whole thing was a billion-to-one miracle.

"The mistake wasn't noticed until the following day, and during examination of the sick rabbit the researchers noticed an improvement in it. But we didn't have any proper blood work or history on this rabbit, so they got another rabbit with tumors, ran test on it, and gave it the high blood pressure medication.

"Within a day the tumors had shrunk in size and the blood results showed an amazing turn around. By the end of the week, the rabbit was cancer free. It was an absolute miracle." Neal lowered his head and gave a small laugh.

"What's funny Neal?" Maurice asked.

"The funny thing was, was the drug didn't have any real effects on high blood pressure." Neal lifted his head and continued. "When we found out, we were very careful. We did numerous tests on animals and the results were amazing. In every single animal study we did we saw a reduction in the cancer or a cure. Of course, there was a point of no return, where there was too much damage done by the cancer to be able to help the animal.

"We kept things very secretive. We would conduct blind studies having one set of researchers deal with the sick animals, give the animals treatment, and then we would have a second set of researchers, sometimes in a different country do the results. That way one team wouldn't know what the other was doing and we wouldn't have an information leaks.

"After nine months we secretly tested on humans. We would go down to third world countries and find patients. Many patients had poor or no medical files—it was very easy to cover up what we were doing. We studied on brain cancer, ovarian, prostate, pancreatic you name it. The results were... well I know I said it before: 'it was a miracle'."

"Hallelujah," said Maurice.

<Laughter and screams>

Neal gave a sheepish grin and continued. "We even tried other human experiments. We would treat a patient who had a broken leg, and would give him a dose of the formula. The following day we would inject the same patient with cancer. The resulting blood work showed he was cancer free. We had a cancer vaccine that was a cure and a preventative! It would change the history of the world!"

"Why doesn't the world know about it?"

"Darryl told us to shelve it. We made a lot of money with a pharmaceutical division on cancer treatment drugs and it wasn't financially viable."

"But think of the money you could make selling this vaccine. You could treat billions, and make money hand over fist and be considers heroes. The world would have put you on a pedestal," suggested Maurice.

"Darryl said we can make more money off the sick than the healthy. Only a small portion of the world could actually afford this type of medicine. Third world countries couldn't afford it, and if we refused treatment to people because they couldn't afford it, we would have been raked over the coals in the press.

"If you did the math, and trust us we did, it was more profitable to sell the cancer treatment medication we had, then selling the cure. It was strictly a business decision."

"But think of the fame," suggested Maurice. "Your names would have been celebrated and remembered. You could have been more beloved than Dr. Jonas Salk. Your company could have been the worlds golden child."

"Darryl is no Jonas Salk."

"You bastard!" Darryl yelled out again. "We saved your dying wife with that formula. You injected yourself with it too! You will *never* get cancer you idiot! It's just the world isn't ready yet! It isn't ready!" Darryl just happened to forget to mention, he took the formula as well as members of his immediate family.

"We kept a small amount of the formula around. If you had the money available, we could help. If you were sick and poor like the majority of the world is —well, the bottom line isn't as profitable as you would think." Neal looked over at Darryl. "I'm just as guilty as you," and he lowered his eyes to the floor.

"Thank you Neal," Maurice said with a smile. "Thank you for telling the truth. Now it is time for the consequence!"

<Applause and screams>

Out of Maurice's back pocket he brought out a small tube with a greenish, red liquid.

<Ohh's, awe's and screams>

Maurice raised the liquid in front of his eyes. "Inside this is the deepest part of hell. Pain, suffering and torment. A second of this will seem like a lifetime, with only lifetimes of limitless pain to follow. Only reserved for a select few." Maurice turned to Darryl. "You are our grand prize winner." Darryl wanted to scream but it was lost in his voice. But instead of walking towards him, the game show host gave the tube to Neal who without hesitation lifted the contents to his mouth and swallowed.

Immediately blood seeped from his eyes and he fell straight to the ground. Darryl knew Neal wasn't dead. He was alive just like Eddie and Carrie.

"A special thank you to our guests and thank you for playing Truth and Consequences!"

<Applause>

There was a flash and all three found themselves sitting in a well-furnished room. Darryl, looked beside him on sitting on the plush couch was Linda and Brian. They looked back at him with equal confusion. Nobody said a word and the door to the room opened. An attractive young woman wearing a headset and carrying a clip board walked into the room. "Copy that, three minutes," she said into the headset.

She looked down at the three. "Please follow me." Like victims from a tornado after the storm leveled their house, they followed aimlessly after the young woman. "Please stand here," as she lined them up behind the curtain. "Copy that, we're going live," she said into the headset.

Live from the seven rings of Hell it's the Truth and Consequence game. And here is your host, Satan!

<Applause>

"Thank you for that lovely introduction Derek."

The three of them looked at each other with confusion and fear.

Darryl peaked past the curtain and saw Eddie, Carrie and Neal all alive and healthy being led from a door on the other side of the stage, making their way to the podiums with nervous smiles.

He walked further back stage and saw a platform being put in place. A stage hand standing next to it was holding a noose in his hand. Confused he walked back to the waiting area. He saw Linda and Brian standing still, but he could see the confusion of their faces.

Next to Brian stood two stage hands that Darryl thought looked familiar. It took him a moment until the horror sank in. It was the same two men who had turned into demons and raped Brian's wife Carrie. As if reading his thoughts they looked over and gave him a little smile.

"Oh fuck he muttered to himself." It was a role reversal. Brian wasn't going like what was in store for him. And the noose was going to be going around Linda's neck this time. For a moment he was wondering what was going to happen to him, then he remembered. The small tube of greenish, red liquid. The words came back to him. *"Inside this is the deepest part of hell. Pain, suffering and torment. A second of this will seem like a lifetime, with only lifetimes of limitless pain to follow. Only reserved for a select few."*

Darryl tried to run, but he mechanically walked back into line behind Brian and Linda. He remembered how Neal without hesitation raised the liquid to his mouth and drank. He knew when his time would come, he would drink without hesitation regardless of how much he tried to fight.

He turned to the woman with the headset on. "We shouldn't be here! We're not dead! We shouldn't be here!"

The woman with the headset gave a little smile. "Oh, you silly! Of course you're dead! You're all dead! I'll give you a heads up. Down here time doesn't work like it does on Earth. When your new friend gets ass fucked by those demons and the lady over there starts swinging by her neck... well time goes real, real slow," she said twisting a curl in her hair with a finger.

"Lifetimes will pass. And you... well... when you take a drink of that liquid, you'll wish you were hanging from your neck getting ass fucked by two demons. And you'll repeat this whole game over and over and over..." she said with a sweet smile.

They could hear Maurice's smooth voice on the other side of the curtain.

"Let's not waste any time now, shall we. Our first contestant is a truck driver, he is 51 years old and his name is Edward. Let's hear it for Edward."

<Applause>

The smiling young lady with the headset on turned her attention to Linda and tapped her on the shoulder. "You'll be up soon. Have fun out there!"

The Waiting Room

Stephen stopped outside of the office. He looked up at the building, it was white of course, he didn't expect anything less. He stood there for a moment fidgeting, playing things out in his mind. Did he really want the answers to his questions? Maybe he should just wait until tomorrow. But Stephen knew he couldn't wait. If he were to turn around, chances were he would never return. He took a breath, opened the door–and stepped into God's waiting room.

The waiting room was exactly how he pictured it, painted a soft white with beautiful, soothing paintings on the wall. In the corner was a beautiful oak desk with a pretty, young woman behind it. She must be God's receptionist. Stephen slowly walked up to the desk and gave her a little smile.

The young lady smiled back and asked warmly, "Can I help you?"

"Umm, hi. Ah, I was wondering if I could... maybe if he had time and wasn't busy... umm am I allowed to see him?" he embarrassingly muttered out.

"See God?" she asked.

"Ahhh, ya. I mean yes."

"Do you have an appointment?" she asked looking down at the appointment book in front of her.

"I didn't know I needed an appointment, sorry. Should I come back another time?"

She flipped a couple of pages. "No, no. He's in a meeting right now but does have some free time on his schedule. Do you want to take a seat Mr. Hastings?"

He was going to ask her how she knew his name, but this was Heaven, nothing should surprise him anymore. He thanked her and took a seat. When he sat down, he let out a small gasp. He just sank into the chair and it seemed to hug his body. It was the most incredible feeling. The chair seemed to adjust to the body's needs and attuned itself perfectly. He gave a little sigh and relaxed further into the chair. Any hesitation and anxiety he had about meeting God, melted away in the chair.

Stephen died about three weeks earlier. He was sitting at his computer when he had a brain aneurism and was dead before his body hit the floor. He didn't remember much of what happened next. It was like waking from a dream he was standing in a mist when things slowly started coming into focus.

He felt something brush against his legs and jumping up on him. He looked down in confusion and saw an extremely excited collie. He immediately recognized the animal, it was Morty, the dog he had as a child. He kneeled and started to pet and hug him. He didn't even notice the tears in his eyes.

Another dog came up to him, followed by another. Rollie! Baley! Dogs he owned as an adult. He hugged them all when he heard a familiar voice behind him. It was impossible— he turned around and saw Beverly. He let out a giant sob and rushed into her arms. He kept crying while she petted his hair and soothed him.

"It's okay. I've been waiting a long time for you," as she hugged him closer.

He let out another wet sob. Beverly his wife, had died at the age of 35. She was killed in a car accident, the victim of a drunk driver. The drunk behind the wheel didn't have a scratch on her, but his wife was taken away from him.

They had been married nine years. Nine of the best years of his life. He was absolutely devastated by her death. He barely had the strength to go on, but he had somehow managed. He wouldn't have made it if it wasn't for... his thoughts were interrupted with more voices.

He looked up from Beverly's shoulder and saw his parents with big smiles on their faces and joined in the hug. He even noticed Gary Renny, his childhood best friend who died of cancer at the age of 10. He looked exactly the same as he remembered him when he was healthy.

Stephen found out later that when you cross over, pets are usually the first to greet you. It's less of a shock then seeing a loved one right away. He hugged and kissed so many people he hadn't seen for such a long time. They laughed and shared living memories. Beverly explained that he had died, and he was now in Heaven. It would take some time to adjust; God liked to give people their own time to transition from the mortal to the immortal life.

Heaven was whatever Stephen wanted. He could choose to live in his childhood home, his first apartment, his dream house. Anything he wanted was his.

There was a lot of nature in Heaven. Beautiful snow-capped mountains surrounded by beautiful tall trees. Crystal blue lakes with miles of enormous coniferous and deciduous trees. His house was in the middle of a mid-sized village, something out of a Swiss 1960's tour book. In the middle of the village stood a beautiful Victorian weather worn building that was a local university.

Students were playing Frisbee and football on the front grass, while study groups sat under trees and couples walked hand and hand across the fresh cut grass. It was perfect because it was Heaven of course.

When he was alive Stephen was an astrophysicist. He loved gazing up into the sky, staring at the stars and contemplating the mysteries of the universe. He never like going into the city, the noise always seemed amplified and the buildings claustrophobic. Life away from the city was freeing, cleaner, and since he felt socially awkward, he enjoyed the solitude. In his Heaven he was surrounded by nature which he always admired and wished he could have spent more time in when he was alive. His neighbours were some of his best friends and colleagues, all of whom had passed. Heaven was only available to the dead.

He loved the university. Some of his greatest memories were going to school and sitting in the lecture halls. Years after his graduation, his career was lined with professional success and acknowledgments, he loved stepping back into universities. Visiting as a colleague to work on a new theory or as a guest speaker and accepting a teaching job later in his life, the smells and memories came rushing back. Just the sounds of his feet echoing off the marble floors in an empty hall would make the hairs on his arms stand up.

Each day in Heaven, he would walk over and sit in some lectures held by Galileo Galilei or a Q&A with Stephen Hawking. Other lectures were held in philosophy, art and music. The art department had an enormous building with some of the greatest artist who ever lived. Rembrandt, Van Gogh, Michelangelo and countless other masters. Stephen could walk into a lecture hall, having the best seat in the house and watch the artist create his work, describing his techniques and talking about any problems or doubts they encountered during the creation of the original masterpiece.

There was no concern about missing a lecture, because he knew it would always be there when he wanted it. He could browse the enormous library, which put every library on earth to shame making them look like a book kiosk in comparison.

In the distance there was a mountain and he noticed a giant observatory on the peak. He knew when he wanted to visit, he would climb into a jeep that would be waiting in his driveway, find a dirt road out of the village, and wind his way up the mountain until he came across the observatory. It would be filled with the most amazing equipment and give a spectacular view of the heavens.

A view of the heavens from Heaven. Stephen frowned and shifted slightly in his seat. Just when he thought his seat could not feel any more perfect, he was wrong. He let out a small moan of comfort and he saw the secretary look over at him with a smile on her face, and she continued with her work.

For the entire walk over to God's office he tried to figure out what he was going to say. Yet, here he sat only feet away from the door which God was behind, and he had no idea how to even start the conversation.

He was distracted from his thoughts when the door to the waiting room opened and a man walked in. He had a very peaceful look on his face–but so did everyone else in Heaven. He was wearing a beautiful white suit with a light green tie with yellow smiley faces on it. Normally a clash of green and yellow would be a fashion faux pas, but in this man's case it worked, and the tie brought a smile to Stephen's face.

"Good morning Jina," the man said as he turned towards Stephen and made his way to the chair beside him. "Good morning No," Jina the secretary replied.

The man sat in the chair beside Stephen and he recognized the sound of bliss coming from the man as he sat down. "Comfortable aren't they?" Stephen asked with a knowing smile.

The man returned the smile, "They're the best seats in town my friend." The man offered a hand and Stephen shook it. He was impressed with the power in the grip. The man was about 3 inches shorter than him and at least 100 pounds less. In his previous life the man could have been a jockey.

"My name is No," the man offered.

"Stephen."

"I can always tell a new comer when I see one. How long have you been in Heaven Stephen?"

"Three weeks," he replied with some surprise. "How could you tell that I'm new?"

"It's all in the eyes my new friend. Much like when we were alive, you could tell something about a person's eyes. Of course, it is much easier here in Heaven. The one advantage is no one is trying to project a different image or cover up lies. It's quite easy actually."

"How long have you been here?"

"A long time Stephen, a long time." Nothing was said for a moment, and Stephen believed that was the end of that. But No shifted in his seat and let out another little moan of pleasure and continued.

"I died 2400 years, 75 days, 23 minutes and exactly 7 seconds ago." No looked over to Stephen with a little grin. He laughed when he saw the expression on Stephen's face. "When you're here as long as I have, you'll be able to pull up exact answers as well."

"How did you die?" asked Stephen before he could catch himself. He turned red with embarrassment and apologized. "Oh my god, I'm so sorry. That's a terrible thing to ask." His face flushed again when he caught what he said. "I didn't mean to say 'Oh my god' either. I meant no offence." He looked over at Jina the secretary and she still had her head down working on something.

No gave a small laugh and gave Stephen a little pat on the hand. "It's okay my friend. You're not offending God or anyone else with that; and the one thing about Heaven is that everyone who is up here has died. It's not a big deal.

"On Earth I was born a slave and I died a slave. When I was young, I was taken away from my mother when I was two. Our masters would separate children from their families and constantly move children from compound to compound. Children were never shown any affection shown to them, nor were they ever taught to speak.

"I found out when I arrived in Heaven that the reason, was that our masters wanted slaves to be robotic. Thousands of years before robots were even conceived; they wanted their slaves to just focus on their tasks. They would have no connection to any fellow slaves around them, and it they believed it would be impossible to talk about a revolt, if nobody could talk.

"They were fools in their thinking. Many elders would secretly try to teach the young and if that didn't work, we learned basic sign language. Plus, the masters had a terrible time explaining what they wanted us to do, since many could not understand.

"I was one who never learned to speak and had to rely on hand gestures to communicate. When I was a young boy I remember playing with another child. We were playing some nonsensical game and when it was my turn, he would point at me and say, 'No! No!' No didn't have any meaning to it, like it does in the English language, but I adopted the sound as my name and have kept it ever since."

Stephen listened to No talk about his life. It didn't seem like much of a life. He spent his days being told what to do–farm, tend to animals, building, repairing–whatever his masters wanted. He studied No's face looking for anger or resentment. There was nothing– maybe he got over it with time or maybe it was being in Heaven that took away the resentment.

Stephen never felt better than he did in Heaven with a constant warm, happy feeling inside. He thought about his life and thought back to moments where he used to hold his anger. One of the people he used to hate was a man named Glen Enos. Glen was a former classmate and research partner.

They worked for two years together before things blew up between them in the span of three days. They were working on a paper that Stephen believed to be incomplete, but Glen deemed it complete. He removed Stephen's name from the paper and took credit for the work himself. Not to be outdone, slept with his girlfriend the following day.

It turned out to be a blessing in disguise because he met Beverly a month later and fell intensely head over heels in love. But he always hated Glen. Sleeping with his girlfriend was bad but stealing work and not giving credit was inexcusable. It helped a small bit that when the paper was reviewed, it was panned because it was deemed rushed and incomplete. Nonetheless, he held onto the hate until the day he died.

But in Heaven it didn't bother him. But there was a huge difference in losing a girlfriend and being betrayed by a friend compared to being a slave. To be separated from loved ones, to be kept ignorant of knowledge and to be beaten as a form of motivation – that was like comparing Earth to the known universes largest celestial object VY Canis Majoris. Even with comparisons his mind was in space.

"I remembered the day I died," No said winding down his story. "We were herding some goats when one of our masters on horseback was yelling at me. He was pointing over to the river. I had no idea what he was saying, I thought maybe he wanted a drink, I didn't know.

"He got out his whip and lashed my back. I was panicking not understanding what he wanted when I saw that a goat had wondered off and was headed towards the river. I started to run over when he lashed out again. The whip caught the side of my head and I collapsed. I heard muffled yells and could feel more lashes opening up my back, but I couldn't move. I don't think I was on the ground long, maybe only seconds; but it felt like I was in a dream.

"I managed to get up and get out of the way of his whip. My vision was blurred, but I could see the river. I had no idea where the goat was, my eyes weren't focusing very well; I just hoped they would clear up the closer I got.

"My feet were very unsteady, and I was vomiting as I ran. I guess my master feared that the goat was going to be washed away by the water. Well as fate would have it, I saw the goat–blurry, but I could make out its shape. My head was pounding, and I felt sick to my stomach, but I had managed to stop vomiting.

The goat started to turn right but I staggered left, out of control. I didn't even know I was in the water until I noticed I couldn't breathe. Another thing I couldn't do was swim. As I drowned in the river, the goat wondered back to the other goats and they continued on their way.

"The master never attempted to save me or send anyone to help. I was just another slave to them, less important than a goat."

Although the thought of being less than a goat, No never lost the cheerfulness in his face or in his eyes. The life he had led was in the past, and he was now living in the now–living in paradise.

"What are you hear to talk to God about," Stephen asked.

"Me? Nothing. I've never met God. I just like to come in here and sit in these fantastic chairs. It's a wonderful feeling, being comfortable in this chair knowing he's just on the other side of the waterfall."

Stephen couldn't mask his confusion. There were no waterfalls anywhere around here as far as he knew, and the room had some beautiful art on the walls, but none of them were waterfalls.

"What waterfalls No?"

He casually raised he right hand and pointed to the wall to the right of Stephen. He looked over and studied the wall in confusion.

"What do you see?" asked No.

"Just a plain white wall." Stephen answered unsure of what was going on.

"I see a beautiful waterfall. Quiet enough to be able to hear you and with a gentle mist that occasionally comes from it and cools my face."

No looked around the room and looked back to Stephen. "Heaven is what you want it to look like. How was the weather outside for you?"

Again, he was confused, but answered the question. "Beautiful. The sun was out, a slight breeze, with a couple of fluffy, white clouds in the sky. It's... well...perfect."

No smiled. "For me it's raining. I *love* the rain. Sometimes it's a downpour which I love going for long walks in and sometimes it will just be a gentle mist. There are days of course when it's nice out, I enjoy the sun too, but rain is my favorite."

No looked at Stephen with a big smile on his face and asked, "What am I wearing?" No laughed and especially loved the description of the tie. "See, in my Heaven I'm naked. I'm naked sitting here talking to you. You're naked and Jina over there is naked too. Everyone in my Heaven is naked.

"You see, this is part of my Heaven. The weather, the people around me and even this office is how Heaven looks to me. You have a beautiful sunny day, with me wearing a funny tie. Everything in Heaven looks the way you always imagined."

No saw a troubled look on Stephen's face and that was a very rare site in Heaven. "Why are you here my friend? Why did you come to see God?"

Stephen looked around the room, down at his feet and back to No. "I'm not supposed to be here. None of this. Me, you, Jina" he said nodding towards her. "None of this is supposed to be here. God isn't supposed to be here."

"I don't understand my friend," No said in a caring voice.

"I don't believe in God. I'm a man of science and when I was alive, I was an atheist. I didn't believe in Jesus, Mohammed any of the deities. There was no Adam and Eve, we were formed through evolution.

"The idea of Heaven is a comforting idea to tell a child when a grandparent or their hamster died. When I died that was supposed to be it. Gone, done. I would simply cease to be.

There would be no afterlife and no reincarnation. It was supposed to be a one and done deal, but here I am."

No remained silent and let Stephen talk.

"I'm not saying I'm not happy. I am! It's truly beautiful here. And Beverly! I missed her so much. When she passed I was devastated. I couldn't stop crying for days upon days; and when I stopped, I felt dead inside. I wanted to cry again because at least I would be feeling or at least appearing to feel something."

Stephen could no longer look at No. He just stared down at his hands and took a moment to collect himself. It appeared that even though he has lost his anger towards Glen Enos, he apparently could still remember the pain when he lost his wife.

"When I lost her, I came close to losing myself. Even though I didn't believe in God, I used to lay in bed every night and pray for God to kill me. A simple bolt of lightning hitting me though my bedroom window or to squeeze my heart so I could have a heart attack.

"The only thing that kept me from killing myself was my work. Beverly would always joke that science was my mistress." He looked back up to No, knowing that he had to be honest. Totally honest.

"Work saved me... and so did Aimee. For a couple of years after Beverly passed, I was consumed with my work. I would spend hours upon hours working on theories and formulas. I never noticed the concerned look from my colleagues; and when they would start to say something out of concern, I would quickly defuse it and change the subject."

A smile appeared on Stephen's face. "I met Aimee at a barbeque. My next-door neighbour was having one, and I had just pulled into my driveway and he was taking something out the trunk of his car. He invited me over saying that the burgers were on the grill and there were plenty of cold beers just waiting to be opened.

"In truth, the only reason I said yes was because I was hungry and didn't feel like cooking or waiting to have something delivered and the thought of a nice cold beer sounded good too. It was great timing on my part, it was really crowded... so I figured nobody would see me come in, grab a bite and slip out."

He nodded hello to a few people, stood around with some people talking and discreetly slipped away to be by himself. There was a table set up near the fence with bins filled with ice, keeping cold numerous beers, sodas and waters. Just like something out of a cheesy romantic movie he reached in for a drink at the exact time someone else reached in. They touched hands and when he looked up, he saw a beautiful woman, wearing a floral summer dress and a light pink summer hat.

Stephen didn't know what to say and took him a few seconds to realize they were both still holding hands. They both laughed from embarrassment and struck up a conversation. Her name was Aimee, a divorcee with a son in his second year of college. She used to work as a photographer for National Geographic, travelling the world.

It was difficult work because she was away from her family a lot of the time. Possibly one of the reasons for her failed marriage or possibly an excuse for her husband's numerous affairs. She now worked as a freelancer and was able to pick and choose her assignments. Her life had always been busy and now she was enjoying the quiet pace of having a routine. The two talked for hours and were one of the last the leave the party.

Out front by her car, Stephen felt something. He had been isolated with his work for so long, he had forgotten what it felt like to be around a woman. A woman who made his stomach do flips when she would smile; a woman who made him blush when she teased him. A woman who sent a hot current through his body when she touched his arm while laughing at something he said.

Completely out of character for him he lowered his defenses and was very direct. "I don't want you to leave," he said as she looked quizzically into his eyes. "I can't bear the thought of you driving away. I want you to stay. I need you to stay."

Completely out of character for her she replied, "I want to stay."

It was a love that Stephen thought was impossible. Colleagues noticed a difference right away. There was something new about him. His eyes seemed brighter, they could tell he was in a good mood and when he smiled, they could tell it was genuine.

They married just under a year later. Aimee was an incredible woman, she made him laugh every day and never a day went by where she would come up to him, hug him and look deep into his eyes and tell him that she loved him.

Stephen smiled at No as he told them of the years they had together. How they picked each other up when they were down, and how they loved each other every day 'til the day he died.

Stephen smiled as he talked about Aimee. "This place is simply amazing," he said as he gestured around him. "Heaven truly is... Heaven. Do you know that when I was walking around a few days ago I heard a man playing guitar when I was walking by the park?

"It was an acoustic guitar. It sounded beautiful, but I could tell it was a work in progress because it would stop and start over, sometimes repeating certain parts over or with a slight change in cord progression. It was a man sitting under a tree, looking as relaxed as could be, but totally involved and unaware of everything around him. I walked by and when I got closer, I noticed it was George Harrison picking at the tune, humming the song while he was working on the right notes.

"I had a Beatle sitting only a few feet away working on a song, a song I had never heard before—a *new song* and it was beautiful!" Stephen started to shift in his seat looking more directly at No. "I mean the key to the universe is at my fingertips. I'm surrounded by brilliance every time I enter the university, I have a beautiful telescope on top of a gorgeous scenic mountain that would put any telescope on Earth to shame. I bet, if I wanted, on the other side of the mountain is probably a rocket that will take me out into space, and I could see firsthand the mysteries of the universe. The rocket will probably be piloted by Captain Kirk and he will explain everything to me–either him or Mr. Spock."

No started to laugh and Stephen smiled. "There is no rocket ship for you Stephen." Stephen was confused. It appeared that instead of laughing with him, No was laughing at him. But not in a callous sort of way, this was Heaven after all.

"When you were alive you loved your work, correct?"

"Yes."

"There is no spaceship and that telescope will probably be not much different from the ones you used when you were alive." Stephen was confused. "The brilliant people at the university will help guide and work with you on your continuation of your work on Earth, but no answers will be given to you."

"Why? Why not?"

"Because that would not be Heaven to you."

"Do you love your job? Are you good at it?" No asked.

"It's a passion that sometimes called an obsession. I worked my butt off when I was young to get recognized in my field, and when I was recognized, I worked twice as hard to stay recognized. If I were to lead a presentation to my peers, where I didn't have to dumb it down and get heavy into the math–if I were to go full tilt in my lecture, there would only be a hundred or so people on Earth able to keep up with me and understand what I'm saying."

No smiled at him and didn't say anything right away. He gave Stephen a chance to think about what they had both said. "If you love your job and you are passionate, you are not looking for easy answers and to have things given to you. You want to discover them for yourself."

No was correct. The idea of working beside people he had only read about in history books, to have Einstein pay him a visit one day, would be a total thrill. To work beside men and women everyday who shared his same passion and to learn from them every day was indeed Heaven to him.

Again, he frowned and looked at No. "But it still doesn't explain all of this. As much as I love the idea of Heaven and enjoy being here... I shouldn't, because this shouldn't exist."

No gave him a gentle smile and touched Stephen's hand. "I don't have all the answers for you. Did you find it strange that God's office is so close to you? Only a short walk away. And the man who was playing guitar under the tree? Of all the places he could be, he was in a park so close to you. And me? I said I come here every day, yet this is the only time we have met? In the small town you live in, I imagine you would have recognized me considering the way you see me dressed.

"There are many realms and levels in Heaven. In time you will start to understand."

No rose to his feet and gave a small stretch. "Good bye Jina" he said to the secretary. "Good bye Stephen. Talk to God, he'll have the answers you need."

He watched No leave, but more questions arose in his mind. Over the span of humanity, billions of people have died. So, Heaven could have billions of souls in it. Here he was in God's waiting room, with a single secretary and it didn't even occur to him when he walked in, there were only two chairs to wait in. With the possibility of billions of people here, the waiting room should be the size of a thousand stadiums.

No had mentioned realms and levels. Stephen wondered when No walked into the waiting room everyday just to enjoy the amazing comfortable chairs, would there be only one seat in the office?

"God will be with you shortly Mr. Hastings," Jina said with a smile from behind her desk.

"Thank you," he said returning the smile.

When he sees God should he bow? Or maybe drop to one knee? Do the sign of the cross?

He heard the office door open and he glanced over. He was shocked to see Beverly standing at the entrance. "Bev? What are you doing here?"

"I was going to ask you the same question," Beverly said with a concerned look on her face. "Did you forget about your party?"

Funny enough he did. It seems even in Heaven you can be forgetful; or maybe that is one thing that will eventually fade over time. All his relatives and friends who had passed were going to have a big party for him. Such a party on Earth, not with dead family and friends of course, would have been a form of punishment. But, in Heaven, it seemed– perfect. He asked for a little bit of time so he could acclimatize himself to Heaven before having the party. And today was the big day and here he was waiting to talk to God about how none of this was possible.

"I'm sorry, hon. I actually did forget. I hope I didn't ruin everything."

Beverly gave a small laugh which made his heart flush in love hearing that wonderful sound he had missed for so long. She touched his hand, another flush and the hair on his arms stood up. How he had missed her touch too.

"You're not going to ruin anything in Heaven Stephen," she said. "But I can tell something is bothering you. What is it?"

He didn't want to upset her, but she was owed the truth. "I shouldn't be here Bev." He gestured around him. "This shouldn't be here, you shouldn't be here."

"How can an atheist be in Heaven?" she said with another beautiful smile. "Oh honey, I've seen it on your face since you first got here. I could see the conflict going on in your head, but stubborn old Stephen wouldn't talk about it; you just had to try to figure things out on your own. I'm not surprised you ended up here to talk to God and debate him about his existence."

Stephen couldn't help but smile. "How did you know I was here?"

"Honey," she said. "It's Heaven."

She took his other hand and drew him closer to her. "I know that's bothering you and it will be your journey to figure out. You're not the first atheist in here. I will help you as much as I can; but that's not why I'm here. We were together for a long time and I know you very well. I can see something is bothering you. I can see it every time you look at me and every time you touch me." She looked at him with her soft eyes and he fell in love with her all over again. A tear traced down his check. "What is it?"

Stephen could feel warmth engulfing him. He had a peaceful feeling ever since entering Heaven and it was stronger now. He had no doubt it was coming from God on the other side of the waiting room door.

"Aimee," he said.

"Oh Stephen," she said and pulled him into a warm hug. When they drew apart there were more tears on his face and a loving smile on Beverly's. "My love, I know how much pain you were in when I left you. I felt your hurt and what you were going through. I also know what Aimee did for you.

"I love her so much for what she did for you. I love her for loving you and making you happy again. I was so happy for you when you found love again, and I look forward to the day when she arrives here, I can give her a hug and thank her in person."

Stephen couldn't talk over his sobs and Beverly continued. "How can you live with both of us without feeling you are hurting one of us?" He could only nod to her. "You can live eternity with her just the two of you—and you can do the same with me."

She could see the confusion on his face. "You are in Heaven. You can be divided many times and live countless lives at the same moment. I know the scientist in you will struggle to find out how and why, but you will learn to do it with ease."

"There are many realms and levels in Heaven," he said repeating No's words.

Beverly smiled at that. "Your life with Aimee is just as important as your life with me. I would never rob you of loving her again. There is no jealousy and there is no envy.

"When you remarried, I was *so* happy for you. I could see the love for her in your eyes, just as I can see the love for me in them right now."

He drew her in for a kiss and a long hug. "You are an amazing woman," he said as he wiped his eyes dry.

"I know," she said with a smile.

"Excuse me, Mr. Hastings?" Jina's voice spoke out from behind them. "God is available to see you now."

Stephen looked at the door leading into God's office. He hadn't seen anybody leave. Maybe there was another exit, or maybe God didn't have an earlier appointment. Was No's appearance a coincidence? Were there any coincidences in Heaven?

Stephen starred at the door and looked back at Beverly. He gave her a smile. "Sorry Jina. I'll have to reschedule some other time. I have a party to go to."

Stephen and Beverly both laughed and walked hand and hand out of God's waiting room.

Chaos in B Minor

The following is the official confession of Alexander Harlan at Rollins-Loch Penitentiary. I write this in sound mind and body.

Numerous times I have been asked for a confession of my crimes. The police demanded one and seemed rather disappointed when I pleaded guilty without as much as saying good morning to them. My lawyer asked for my side of the events but I refuted him, only telling him I was guilty of the charges against me and when I was sentenced to death I refused to appeal it. I know the families of my victims want to know the truth as well as my fans around the world as do the pigs in the media.

I write this with a promise from Father Wade Humber–the priest of Rollins-Loch Penitentiary that he will release it after my execution on the 19th of September. I know I won't answer all the questions that people have of me. I am a man of many flaws–my ego above all. My desire for success over humanity and compassion is inexcusable. Even knowing that, I will leave out a lot of the details of my life in this confession.

Even this close to death, I can't fully open up about my childhood. There will be books written about me that can cover it, and a lot has been unearthed since my crimes. Regardless, the only thing people want to hear about is the blood and the thoughts of a murderous genius. The childhood of a musical prodigy is less interesting. Nonetheless, I will touch on my childhood briefly.

There was music in my house when I was young–it just wasn't played. We had a big stereo in the living room. The kind that was made to be part of the furniture. A long wooden unit that opened at the top exposing the turntable, controls and an area for the records. We had Count Basie, Howling Wolf, Marvin Gaye, Rolling Stones and other greats.

I assume the stereo was my mother's because my father seemed to hate music. He never played it in the car. Instead we I had to listen to a steady drone of talk radio. I'm not sure why my father disliked music. If it was played in the house he would yell at me to turn it down. At one point in her life my mother enjoyed music, but she stopped. But I think something inside of her broke. I don't know if it was my father that broke her or my birth.

I'm not saying it was because of me; I mean post-partum depression. Whatever the answer, when I see old photos of her, I can see joy and the love of life in her eyes. Eyes filled with excitement and dreams, something I had never seen firsthand. Well, regardless—whether it was my father's constant complaining and berating or the chemical and hormonal imbalance from birth—my mother walked out on us when I was six years old. I was told she moved to Colorado—I never saw or heard of her again. To this day I have no idea if she is alive or dead.

I don't think you have to be a psychiatrist to figure out that this must have had some effect on me. Did it lead me to murder? Probably not. I could make it an excuse, and maybe some doctors would say her abandonment stunted my emotional growth. It was my ego and passion for success and perfection that made me a murderer.

When my mother left, I spent a lot of time in my room listening to my small radio. It was safer up there, away from my father. Mother leaving added to his hostility and I quickly learned if I didn't want to be the focus of his anger, it was best to stay away from him.

I found sanctuary in my closet with my radio. I would shut my bedroom door and sit in the closet–door closed so Father couldn't hear–and just soak up the music. The radio had a soft blue glow coming from its dial and cast a small aura around the radio. Even to this day, if I'm having a bad day, I just remember the beautiful blue glow and the magical sounds that used to come out of its tiny speakers.

There was so much music with a simple turn of a dial. I loved rock and roll and the energy that it had. I discovered some country music that I appreciated, but some of it was lazy in my opinion. Jazz! Now that was far from lazy. I loved it! People who think of me now automatically think of me as a racist, but far from it. I loved black music. Jazz, Soul, the Blues and the magic of Motown. It had me hooked right away. Looking at my mother's albums she'd left behind, it was probably the only thing we had in common.

Turning the radio dial was always an adventure. You never knew if you were going to be thrilled with a new song or disappointed by a commercial. I can't remember the name of the first classical piece I heard but I certainly do remember the feeling.

The sound was organized chaos. So many different instruments working as one. My stomach did a turn as if I was on a roller coaster. It was so exciting and more importantly it felt familiar. When I heard the horns and the strings mixing together, I knew that this was what I was supposed to do. This was my destiny–I had found the meaning of my life.

I think I am done with writing about my childhood. There are more sordid details in interviews and books that have been written about me. Nobody reading this wants to know about me being discovered in grade four as a child prodigy. They just want to know how a musical genius became a child murderer and a cop killer.

The term musical genius is thrown around a lot these days. Do I consider musicians such as Bruce Springsteen and Elton John geniuses? Absolutely. They heard the music in their head and they were able to play it and be successful. What about Elvis? Fuck no. He just sang the songs. He never wrote a damn thing. If he received co-writing credits it was all phoney. The label insisted his name was put on those songs. He was a successful singer but genius? Far from it.

Am I a musical genius? Yes. Regardless of what I have done, give me credit for my music. I've always heard music in me and I've been blessed to be able to turn those sounds into notes on paper. I always knew how the wind instruments sounded in front of the brass and with the strings having a life of their own. I could hear the percussions in the back wanting to bust through and everything being guided by a piano. Magic does exist and to call it forth you must master its eighty eight keys.

I released my first album in 1998 entitled *Good morning, Midnight*. The critics and public liked it. Sales exceeded expectations, which won me over with my record label. I was pleased with it, but like any artist, I knew I could do better. I knew I had more in me, but at the time that was the best I could do. I never allowed myself to be beaten down with self-doubt and pity. I had to build on my success and grow as an artist.

The following year I released *Balloons on the Moon*. It proved to everyone that I was no flash in the pan. My fan base blossomed around the world and I had requests to play in gorgeous theatres. The fame was exciting; the money was welcomed but the pressure was on.

My third album *had* to be huge. I believe my record label would have been content with an album that was as successful as *Balloons on the Moon*, but I wanted more. I needed more. I spent months in my condo that overlooked the city skyline, searching for inspiration hidden within the keys of my piano.

Nothing seemed good enough. There were some pieces that were beautiful; but they didn't have the '*it*' factor. I had one small section that had great tempo, but I couldn't work anything around it. Ford was looking for some music for its commercials for a new truck line that was coming out. My agent let them listen to the small piece I had and they ended up buying it.

I don't care if the music purists say that I sold out. I did. I sold out and made a boat load of money and a free Ford pickup every year for the next 20 years. The income took the pressure off having to rush my new album. If it took a few years to do, then fine. When I was happy with it, then it would be ready.

But everything changed one day. It changed the direction of my music and the direction of my life. I woke up early on a Tuesday morning around 5 am and started to work. I wasn't usually an early morning person; but I was experimenting. Like a mad scientist I tried making music late at night. I tried afternoons and mornings. I would play with all the lights off or the next week with different coloured light bulbs to see if that triggered inspiration in me. I used sleep deprivation to see what that would do. The music was interesting, but nothing I would release.

I was looking for my *Sargent Peppers*. Some of the material I was getting was really good; but I was being extremely picky, looking for perfection. I played for about three hours before putting on the kettle and making myself a coffee. I sat down and was watching morning television when it was interrupted. An airplane had hit one of the World Trade Center buildings in New York. I knew New York very well and I was stunned seeing this massive building pouring out black smoke.

The reporters said a plane hit the Tower and they were trying to find witnesses to the accident when in the corner of the TV screen another plane–a passenger plane came roaring in and slammed into the other Tower. The 9/11 attacks seemed like a crazy Hollywood movie or video game come to life. The numbing images of people jumping to their death, to the sudden collapse of both towers.

The attack on the Pentagon and the crash of another airliner in an empty field felt like the world had gone crazy. Every minute I sat there, I was expecting to hear about another attack. I became very aware of my condominium and that I was on the top floor. I would glance out hoping I wouldn't see a plane plummeting towards me.

After a few hours I was exhausted and turned off the TV. The craziness seemed to numb me. I felt physically and mentally tired. I looked out my window and looked upon the city. Everything was so normal here, but in New York, it was a war zone.

I sat down at the piano, not intending to go back to work. The piano always brought me comfort and that was what I was looking for. Without trying I just started to play when something suddenly came out. The energy and emotion of the piece gave me goose bumps while I played. One of my biggest hits: 'Fragments' was born. It is hard to believe that such a song was created on 9/11. It wasn't a dark piece, far from it. Fans and reviewers described it as powerful and joyous.

When I finished playing my hands were shaking. I wanted to write the music down on paper. I could hear the entire orchestra in my mind and I needed to write it all out. But I couldn't. I had to record what I was doing. I played Fragments again and when I was done, more music was building up just waiting its turn to be released.

I recorded for seven steady hours. When I was finished, I fell onto the couch, drenched in sweat and fell asleep. The attacks and the surge of music exhausted me. When I awoke I was charged full of inspiration and made my way back to the piano. When I felt like I was slowing down, I moved my TV in front of the piano. The replays of the attacks and the smoke that spread over the skyline was my muse.

I was disturbed that something so terrible gave me such inspiration. How could a dark moment bring out such glorious music? You would think that tortured chamber music would come out of me, but on the contrary—it was inspired and electric. I always believed everyone has a little darkness in their soul–I found mine and embraced it. My personal deal with the Devil.

The album the came out of my '9/11 sessions' was a double album entitled *Three*. It was a worldwide hit. My name was included with some of the all-time greats and it was considered by many as the best classical album in the past 100 years.

I of course never told anyone about finding inspiration from misery. I thought I had discovered a gold mine. But I found out that the violence and destruction I watched had a shelf life. Even putting out a double album, I had enough material for another two. I recorded the music and put it away for safe keeping for potential use down the road.

A half a year after 9/11, I sat back down behind the piano and rested a lap top nearby with footage of the attack on. The music just didn't seem as powerful as what I recorded on *Three.* The videos no longer had the same effect on me. I wasn't sure if this was a one-time thing, or if I needed new material.

Like a mad scientist I experimented with new videos. I watched beheading videos, people being tortured and killed, deaths caught on video, fatal accidents. My music improved, not quite what I achieved on 9/11, but better than what I released on *Good morning Midnight* and *Balloons on the Moon.*

There was a price to pay for darkening my soul. Sleep was difficult to come by some nights. My dreams were littered with horrific images and no matter how hard I tried to block them, they kept increasing in violence. I thought maybe watching horror movies or action movies might be suitable, but my mind could differentiate Hollywood violence and real violence. My inspiration feasted on *real* violence.

Those close to me noticed a change in me. I was more distant and quiet. I was told I had sad eyes–on one occasion a friend said I had cold eyes. I became more sequestered as my only focus was my music. I had achieved a level of near perfection, and I needed more. I was like a heroin junky–I was chasing that ultimate high.

In 2005 I released *Without Function.* It was a mix of newer material and some of the extra material from my 9/11 session. Again critics and fans fawned over my genius and called it another masterpiece. It was a good album. It was a great album. But it wasn't a perfect album.

I needed inspiration. I needed to see the violence right in front of me. The TV and internet could only do so much. I needed to see the carnage and I needed to hear the chaos. The dark part in my soul had taken over and it drove my music. Nothing mattered more than my work, and I would do anything to fuel its fire.

As I stated earlier, I have no problem saying I am a musical genius–I had proven it. Am I a criminal genius? Absolutely not. I embarrassingly fumbled through my crime with a crazy goal and terrible execution. The goal was simple. I wanted to look past my condo window and below me see the city burn. I wanted to see the flames—to smell its smoke and hear the echoing gun shots. I wanted anarchy and I thought I could be its trigger.

The goal, I thought, was simple. I would cause a race riot. I never occurred to me that Charles Manson wanted to do the same thing in 1969. In my naivety, I thought I could kill some black youths by pretending to be a police officer, then kill a police officer and they'd blame each other for the deaths.

I thought I had it all planned out. For days I played the details in my mind and much like an elite athlete I envisioned my success. For the severity of what I had planned, I should have planned and thought things through longer.

I left a large trail of clues that made it easy for my arrest. The first thing I wanted to do was get a car that would look like an undercover police car. I drove an hour east to rent a car–I thought it was far enough that it would never get traced back to me.

I picked up a dark blue Chevrolet Impala. I thought it looked like a car a cop would drive, I had no idea. I made sure I paid in cash so it wouldn't be traced back to me. Unfortunately I never thought about the copy of my license that the car rental company made. It was the first of many blunders.

My plan, I thought was simple. I was going to shoot down some young black children, leave one as a witness and kill a police officer to make it look like retaliation. I figured tensions would be high on both ends so one little action from either side would light it up like dry kindling.

I didn't want to kill children, but for my plan to work, I had to. If I had killed black teens or adults, there would be anger, but not as much as a child. As much as I would like to say that I fought the idea over and over in my head... I can't. My music meant too much to me. More than a child. More than a grieving parent.

A week before I rented the car I bought a gun at a gun show. I paid cash, made sure I overpaid, so there would be no paperwork. It was the only thing I did right.

On the day of the killing I circled the streets looking for some black children. I had to make sure there weren't any adults around. I avoided schools and parks–too much of a chance of being reported as a suspicious vehicle in the area. I had driven the sedan around for about four hours when I was ready to give up; then I saw them.

There were four black children kneeling on the sidewalk. They were drawing on the concrete with chalk. Kids being kids. I pulled up and quickly jumped of the car. I acted fast before I could chicken out. I was feeling sick to my stomach and my hands were shaking. I didn't want to give myself any opportunity to back out. I *needed* to do this.

I walked up to the children. They were still on their knees looking up from their chalk drawings. I pulled out a fake golden badge from my pocket and I showed it to them. I had picked it up a costume shop the week before. I didn't ask how they were, I just got into my script that I had practiced the night before. "I'm a police officer. I'm tired of you little niggers growing up to be criminals. You all have to die. It's time."

I made sure I mentioned that I was a police officer because at that age they might not understand what a badge was. I started firing and hit the first three children point blank. It was like shooting fish in a barrel. The little boy at the end scrambled and tripped as he tried to get to his feet to run away. I took a step forward and aimed my gun at him. My hands were shaking terribly and I was scared someone would see me so I rushed.

I needed to have a survivor. He needed him to repeat the words I had said. I wanted to shoot him in the leg so he would live. But my shaking hand affected my aim and I shot the child in the lower back. I panicked. I took another step towards him before my mind screamed at me to run.

I bolted to the car, with a painful moan coming from the little boy behind me. The last image I saw of him was him shot in the back, looking over his shoulder at me with eyes wide, full of terror. He crawled on his elbows trying to pull his body away from me. In the last few years of my life, I see those large eyes with tears running from them every night when I try to go to bed.

Heaven only knows how I didn't crash my car. My hands were shaking uncontrollably and tears were running down my face. I was a monster. How could I have possibly done something so horrible? I just remembered the look of confusion on their faces when I pulled out the gun, and the look of fear when I pulled the trigger. I knew I had gone mad and the best thing I could do was kill myself.

But I didn't. I returned the car to the car rental place after getting it washed, just in case any blood sprayed on it. I drove home, removed my clothes (never considering that I just returned my rental and that I could have had blood on my clothes) and put them in a large garbage bag. As I bagged the clothes, I never even noticed I was missing my fake police badge. I had dropped it at the murder scene while I attempted to put it in my jacket pocket.

After throwing the bag containing my clothes down the garbage chute, I had a long hot shower. I kept on questioning myself how I could do such a horrific thing. I wasn't religious but I was convinced I was going to Hell. I stepped out of the shower into a cloud of steam that filled my bathroom. I mechanically dried myself and walked out into the hall like a convict taking his final walk before his execution.

I dragged my feet and had a thousand-yard stare on my face. I shuffled over to the piano and started to play. I felt dead inside but the piano came alive with some of the most beautiful music I had ever played. I sat naked on the piano, my hair still wet, while tears traced down my face. My hands continued to dance across the keys as I cried and cried. I wasn't crying in sadness, it was happiness. The music was gorgeous, everything that I wanted. The children didn't die in vain. Their deaths were the birth of something beautiful.

I went to bed and slept a beautiful deep sleep. I turned on the news and the shooting was the lead story. Two of the children died at the scene and another died on route to the hospital. The child who I wanted to live was rushed to the hospital and they managed to save the little boy's life, but it was unlikely he would ever walk again.

This was upsetting to me. I was hoping the worst that would happen was that the kid would spend the rest of his life with a limp. But now the child would never walk. I was saddened but ... life goes on.

The piece I wrote after killing the children was eventually recorded and released after my arrest to the shock and disgust of many. There are people I trust who want my music to live on, regardless of my actions. I won't reveal any of their names because even after my death, they will still be working for me. The piece was entitled *Picket Fence*–I was visited in prison and asked what I wanted to name the piece. I always joked to myself the bars in my cell were an inmate's picket fence.

Only 500 copies of *Picket Fence* were pressed, all on vinyl. They sold for $300 each.

Of course they sold out right away and copies made it on to the internet. The limited run was just a ploy–a marketing gimmick. I was in the news so much and this just added to the mania. Nobody wanted to like my new music.

The piece was downloaded at last count, 74 million times. I suppose there were some who down loaded out of curiosity and deleted it shortly after. But I guarantee you, that there are a large amount of people who listen to it like a dirty little secret. They know they shouldn't like it considering who made it, but they just can't stop because IT IS BRILLIANT!

You won't hear my music on the radio anymore because of my crimes but if you go into the homes of my critics and fellow composers, they are *all* listening to my work.

After the shooting, I planned my next move. I needed a crappy car. Looking back at it, I guess it didn't really matter what car I had. I overthought it, and again showed my inexperience. I wanted a car that a black person would own. My prejudice assumed it would be a crappy car. I never saw myself as a racist, but probably I am. I don't have the hatred in me like someone in the Ku Klux Klan has. Not even close; but maybe there is a hidden anger or fear in me that brings out racism.

I'm a little too close to the gallows to be worrying about that now.

I used Auto Trader looking for a crap car. There was so much to choose from, but I eventually found my ride. I don't recall the make of the car–I 'm not a car person. All I ever cared about in a car was if it could get me to A to B. Plus, it needed air conditioning. I *always* need air conditioning!

So, this car was a black with a rusted white driver side door. It screamed poor to me, so I paid the guy cash in a quick, hassle-free exchange. This purchase was probably my biggest mistake.

For the next three nights I cruised around the city looking for a police car in an isolated area. It needed to be parked, with the officer hopefully doing paperwork. I saw a couple of times two police cars parked side by side talking, but that would be too risky to shoot at. I needed one car, isolated.

It happened on Friday morning. It was about 2 am when I was driving by a Walmart and saw a police car sitting in the back of the lot, with its headlights on. I slowed my car on the side street beside the parking lot. I could see two officers inside the car. This had me worried. I'd prefer to have just one officer to deal with, but the quiet location was ideal. If I acted quickly, hopefully, I could kill them before they could react.

I pulled into the lot and drove past the front of the car giving them a little wave. I wanted to look like someone who needed assistance, someone who they wouldn't expect an attack. Not only did I give a wave to the officers but unbeknownst to me, I gave a nice little wave to the dash cam. And the cruisers headlights gave me a beautiful spotlight to do my approaching crime in–it sealed my fate before I even killed them in cold blood.

I parked five feet away and started pointing in a direction past the cruiser. I got out of the car stammering and enthusiastically pointing. When they glanced for a brief second in the direction I was pointed, I pulled out my gun and began to fire. The driver's side window imploded as I shot. I was startled by the shattering glass but managed to keep firing inside the car.

When I was just dry clicking the gun I stopped and surveyed the damage. Both officers were slumped in the car, no one moved and there was no groaning or crying noises. I was shocked how well it had worked out. They looked dead and I was unharmed.

In my pocket I pulled out a black fat tip marker and approached the hood of the car.

Unknowingly in full view of the camera I wrote on the hood. "4 the kids. It's time!" I thought it was a cleaver touch adding 'It's time.' When I spoke to the children, I finished with 'It's time' and I thought it would be poetic.

In my mind the black community was certain that a police shooting and the police would suspect that it was a black person who killed their own. Unfortunately for me, the black community never suspected the police. The little boy was very confused trying to remember the shooting and due to the shock and trauma, couldn't remember what I had said.

I had a laundry list of mistakes that led to my arrest. The photocopy of my license I had given to the car rental, the badge I had dropped with my fingerprints on them, matching shell cases with matching finger prints at both scenes, the dash camera showing my face before and after the shootings, along with my writing on the police hood. They even tracked down the owner of the crappy car I bought, the distinguishable black car with rusted white driver's side door. He pointed me out in a police line-up as the person who bought his car.

People assume I plead guilty to my crime because I had no defense–other than insanity.

They say there is a fine line between genius and insanity but I never contemplated it for a moment. Yes, it's true they had me dead to rights; I knew jail was always a possibility and I had to man up for what I had done. Really it comes down to pride. I was embarrassed by how sloppy I handled things.

Another reason I plead guilty was to avoid the families of the people I killed. Well again, I showed my naivety, because before my sentence was handed down members of the families could address me. For nearly an hour and a half grieving loved ones, with anger and hatred, told me about the people I killed. They cried, they screamed and they cursed at me. One of mothers whose child I killed actually forgave me because she said she couldn't live with the hatred and anger because it would destroy her life.

The worst was when the boy I shot and who is now paralyzed from the waist down was pushed to the front of the court in his wheelchair and was turned in my direction while his mother took the stand. She told the court of the dreams her son had of growing up to be a professional baseball or basketball player. How as a little boy, he used to climb all over the furniture pretending the sofa was a mountain and how at the park she would have to keep an eye on him because he loved to climb trees, and if left unsupervised he would climb as high as he could with no fear.

Now instead of climbing he had withdrawn into himself. He is seeing a child psychologist but progress has been very slow. He cries out in the middle of the night screaming out the names of his friends who died around him. While he is being soothed from the nightmare he tells his mother that the bad man is coming back to get him.

The entire time the boy sits in his chair and stares at the back of the courtroom. He is scared of me and doesn't want to make eye contact. After his mother is finished the judge asks the young boy if he wants to say anything to me. For the first time the boy turned his head towards me. He's just a child but the hate in his eyes is obvious. The glare is intense and for a moment I was afraid of him, because he didn't have the eyes of a child anymore–I stole that as well as his ability to walk.

"I hate you." It was the only thing he said than he lowered his head and kept it there while his mother wheeled him away. I don't think the electric chair I will soon be sitting on will hurt as much as the pain I felt at that moment. I wish I killed him, so I can stop seeing him in my mind sitting there, saying those three words.

On my first day in prison, walking towards my cell, I remember hearing the echoes of bar doors being closed and the yells and taunts of other inmates. My first thought was the acoustics were fantastic and imagined the sound that an orchestra could make in such a place; my love of music was still greater than my fear of prison.

Since I was a celebrity I was placed in a special wing, away from the general population. My tiny cell was a far cry from my huge house; but I didn't really care. I had my music still with me–in my head–and I knew this prison had a lot of music hidden it in.

As I've stated, I'm not religious and I'm even less into new age baloney. Modern day hippies talking about people's auras and the spiritual finger prints left behind. I never believed in any of that until I stepped into Rollins-Loch Penitentiary. *Now this place* has an aura to it, and it is cold and dark.

I felt it as soon as I stepped into the prison. You know that chill you get in the middle of your back and you give a little shake to free it? What's that old saying? When a goose walks over your grave? Whatever the saying is, it was like that, but you couldn't shake it free, it just stays with you the entire time.

Talking to fellow inmates many admitted to feeling something 'wrong' about the place as well. The prison had an unusually high suicide rate, almost twice the National average. Even some of the guards who have been to numerous penitentiaries have admitted this place had a very creepy feeling to it.

Rollins-Loch was built in the 1840's. There isn't much of the original prison left; much was knocked down, rebuilt and modified over the years. Some of the original structures remain though unused. The basement in 'C wing' is part of the original prison and is told to have cells down there. It's pretty much a storage area filled with old filing cabinets and desks. I've been told that most guards going down there will usually go in pairs–not for safety reasons, just because they get a strange vibe and most are so scared they feel safer being with someone else.

I've asked several guards and have tried to bribe my way down there. Not because I want to see any ghosts or interest in the paranormal; I just wonder what sort of music I could create going into an area that is feared.

I was also warned by inmates to only talk to the newer guards. The turnover rate in the prison was very high and guards transferred in and out frequently. They say the guards who have been here a long time are hard and brutal. Inmates say they have absorbed the prisons coldness. They are quick to anger and extreme in their violence towards inmates.

I was in my new wing for a short time before I was moved onto death row. Most of the men on the row spent most of their time in their cell with very little interaction other than the other men on the row and the guards who look over them. Of course fame has its benefits.

Warden Garrison is a large man, with an enormous ego. I was taken to his office that was lined with accommodations and plaques. He didn't smile when I entered and never offered a seat. He sat behind a large wooden desk, polished to a glimmering shine. There was a gavel on the desk, probably a reminder to people of who was in charge around here. He read me the riot; act saying that just because of my notoriety; it didn't mean I was to get special treatment. I was to follow the rules and do what I was told or he would come down hard on me. I was on death row waiting to be killed by the electric chair—you couldn't come down much harder than that.

I nodded my head and kept a very serious face. I could tell right away he was a fan of my music. Garrison kept a shit kicker expression on his face, but his eyes gave him away. I had seen that look thousands of times from meeting fans; it's unmistakable. I just had to pretend that he was in charge and I was at his mercy.

It took old Garrison about three weeks until he called me back to his office. He thought it might be a good idea to help morale in the prison if we started a music program. He thought it would be an excellent use of my talent and a chance for other inmates to better themselves musically working with someone of my status.

I told him it was an excellent idea and waited. He had a look on his face, that there was more to be said. He started clearing things on his desk, putting them in his top drawer when he said a matter-of-factly, "Maybe you could even play small concerts for the staff." And there it was. A fan wanted free concerts at his whim. I held in a smile and said, "of course I'd be delighted."

He dismissed me with a wave of his hand, and I knew when the door closed behind me he was smiling to himself thinking he was so clever. I smiled to myself knowing my work could continue.

In my cell I worked at a feverish pitch on beautiful pieces. Granted I didn't have a piano to work them out, but I could hear the music in my head and they came alive on the page. A guard named Henry Dawson worked on Death Row and I would give him a copy of the sheet music for him to give to an unnamed person on the outside. I made sure Dawson was paid handsomely.

I had plenty of money the government didn't know about that trusted people could access and used to pay off guards to retrieve my works. These people on the outside loved my work, and would do anything to hear more of it. They would get a studio recording and hold onto the master tapes for release after my execution. I had money to put for the musicians and the studio time. I also had a lot of investors who would pitch in money with the desire for new music and they would be thanked personally from me with musical piece just for them.

I can't say if the people who produced and engineered the sessions were aware that it was my music. Needless to say I'm quite certain my death tape releases will be big sellers even with the expected public outcry and the victims' families trying to collect from them. The people behind the making of my death tapes know they will get paid first and handsomely for their work. The families would be lucky to get two nickels to rub together from the sales... that's how the music business works.

I had two requests for the warden. First that a piano be set in front of the window in the prison's new music room. I offered to ask for donations of musical equipment from friends, so the prison wouldn't have to take any money out of their budget for the 'warden's music project'. Next was for a keyboard in my cell—with headphones—so I wouldn't be a distraction to my fellow inmates.

Thoughtfully, I would ask for outside donations for this too. It would be a top of the line model that I could record on, mix and play multiple instruments. As I expected the Warden hemmed and hawed over it, but I knew he would agree when I said I could practice my concerts for him and the staff on them. He thought it over for a week before he gave in on the condition that it would be taken away if I misbehaved.

Prison for many is inhumane, a loss of freedom and a very dangerous place. For me I loved many aspects of it. Losing my freedom and moving from a mansion to a shitty little cell takes time to get used to. But my passion for music, which I think I can call an obsession, this was the perfect place. The isolation was what I needed so I could work on things. I wrote earlier about this place having a bad vibe to it... it was like fertilizer for my music. It nourished in the environment I was in and I had never been happier. When I was given my keyboard, I was in heaven just sitting in this tiny cell, with headphones on composing some of my best works.

I knew I had to make friends. I felt pretty safe on the row, but it was better to make friends than enemies. I asked the guard if it was okay for me to play on the keyboard for everybody. If there were any objections I would respect their choice. The guards had no objection thinking it might lift some spirits. They checked with the inmates on the Row and everyone wanted to hear me play.

So for an hour I played some of my favorite pieces. It's strange playing in a small cell, not seeing your audience and hearing only a small amount of applause. I was used to seeing a music hall full of people giving me standing ovations night after night. But I was correct about the prison: the acoustics were wonderful, and although it wasn't a grand piano, my audience appreciated the sound coming from the keyboard.

I performed every Saturday night for the prisoners and guards on the row. I was moved into the hall and chairs were set up for my small audience. I took the performances as serious as if I was performing at the Sydney Opera House. The men deserved some humanity in their lives. I didn't care what crimes they committed. Every person has their reasons for why they did what they did. I grew quite affectionate with the men I shared the row with, and the guards.

I listened to their stories and memories of happier times. I never spoke about my crimes to anyone and was even vaguer about my family. The only time I would light up was talking about music and experiences on the road. I didn't share with them my secrets and the dark side of my inspirations, but I opened up to them in my music. I shared my dreams, my fears and my life in the notes I played and I think over time they started to understand me better.

Starting a music program wasn't terribly important to me. It was a back-up just in case I wasn't allowed anything in my cell. Once they allowed me to have a keyboard in my cell, I couldn't really care less about any music program. But I told myself it was an excellent chance to play with other people again and I had a plan going into it that I was hoping would pay off.

I won't give names of the inmates I met in the program. What started off as a bone that I was throwing the warden, became a huge inspiration for my music. Some of the men I worked with became my protectors and were my contacts to people in general population. They also smuggled out some of my music to my people on the outside. It wasn't that I didn't trust Mr. Dawson who was doing it on the row for me. It was that I was producing so much; I had to split the load. I didn't want Dawson to have too much power over me by being the gate keeper to my legacy. Plus, I doubted very much that Dawson would have set up murders for me too.

One of the smartest pieces of advice came to me on the first day of the program. One of the men who was a very talented musician came up to me when I entered the room. It was a small room, about the size of a classroom. There were some chairs and an impressive assortment of instruments that I had procured for the prison. He started to gush about my music to me and said he even saw me in concert three times. I was impressed with his knowledge and I thanked him for being a fan.

He gently put his hand on my arm and possibly saved me with his advice.

"You need to go easy on these guys. You'll find some talented guys in this place, but they won't be like some of the world class musicians you are used to playing with. They're going to make mistakes and I'm sure they'll make you want to pull out your hair at times.

"But when you yell at a professional for fucking up one of your songs, they shake it off, maybe they're a bit embarrassed , and likely be more angry at themselves for screwing up and they'll practice like a mother fucker to make sure they don't mess up again.

"You try to embarrass or yell at one of these guys, they'll try to beat you to death with their instrument before the guard can get to you and break it up. Treat these men like little children and give them plenty of praise. Help them grow as musicians, but don't think they won't kill you in a heartbeat because a lot of these guys are expecting you to be a rich, pompous, musical faggot."

It was the crude, truthful advice I needed. My only reason going into this music program was for my own needs and gains. I never considered the men who would be in the class with me, nor did I give a shit about them. They were just like the children and the police officers I shot–a means to my musical ends. The advice was absolutely right and probably saved my life.

There were about 20 men in the class and only a few of them knew how to read music. They were terrible. If I hadn't been given that advice I would have had a fit and berated the lot of them. But I just took a deep breath and was very patient because if I didn't I would probably walk into class one day and be greeted with a shank to the neck.

I decided to ditch my plan about playing classical music and decided to go into a direction I thought would be more fun and would hold their attention. I figured after a while if they wanted to give some classical pieces a try we could, but I wasn't going to force anything on them. I thought the Animals; *House of the Rising Sun* would be a good start. The chord progression is pretty simple and it's a great song.

Each prisoner played a song of their choice as an introduction for me to see where they were musically. I gave them plenty of positive feedback and added some suggestions with what I would like to see them work on. When I went back to my cell I would write the music out for each instrument, but instead of using notes I would just write it out A, C, D etc.

But as I mentioned before, I was using this class and these men as pawns for my own game. I needed violence to enhance my music and being locked up with a bunch of violent men is a convenience. Like most people, everyone has a price. In prison you can buy pretty much everything including a murder.

When I requested a piano by the window, I didn't ask it to be placed there so I could gaze out at the clouds. I wanted to see the yard where the men would get a chance to go outside and get some fresh air, work out, socialize whatever a convict does.

When I asked my new friend about hiring a hit, he looked shocked; but he didn't walk away. I wanted a murder to take place on the yard at a certain time, within sight of the window of the music program. I told him I didn't care who it was, the guy who was doing the killing could pick his own target, it didn't matter to me; he just had to agree to the location and the time of the murder.

My friend knew I had money and I assured him I had someone outside who could pay all my 'bills'. I would make sure the money would go to wherever my 'hit man' wanted it— wife, children, girlfriend or drugs that I could get smuggled in. It didn't matter, I could pay up, but my one stipulation was that no one was to know it was me who arranged it. Plus, my friend would be paid handsomely for arranging things.

Well, money sure talks in prison. There were a lot of guys in there facing life sentences who had plenty of men they wanted to ice. The thought of killing an enemy and providing financially for their family at the same time was too good to pass up.

I don't need to get into any mundane details, but let's just say busy was good. I made sure that there was only one murder a month. The music started to flow out of me every time I watched my guy stalk his victim and then strike. Sometimes they would jump on the guy and continue to stab until the guards clubbed him unconscious or sometimes it was a walk by with a quick strike to the neck and continue walking like nothing happened.

I would just sit at my piano and let the music come out. At the time of this confession I have made enough music to record and release for the next 20-years.

The Warden meanwhile used me as his own personal minstrel. Since I was using him, it was only fair he would use me. I don't think he cared much for my musical program. He wanted classical music, something that would be played at Carnegie Hall. He understood the limitations of his prisoners, but he expected world class when it was time for me to play.

I played for him in a room a few doors down from his office. It was probably a conference room, but when I would enter it there were rows of chairs with a baby grand piano at the front. I imagine the piano was probably donated by my contacts it just never made it down to the music program.

Over the years of playing for him, usually once a month, I would enter the room wearing my orange jump suit and walked in silence to my piano while my audience just sat silently getting a good look at a celebrity/murderer. Warden Garrison was always sitting in the front row sometimes with his wife beside him, sometimes it was the Governor or a Senator. He would fill the room with as many powerful, connected people the room could hold.

I would always play my best for the Warden and his cronies, but fuck him if he thought I was going to roll out my hits for him. I would always play pieces that I was trying to work out. Usually they were parts I had trouble working a song around. I would 'jam' on the piano seeing if I could bring life to it or not. Sometimes I could and sometimes I couldn't.

The suits in the audience never knew the difference, as long as this puppet played and it sounded good, that's all that mattered.

I would take my medicine after my performances. I would bow and thank the audience for their kind applause. Sometime I would be made to stand around his cronies and answer questions and sometimes I would be dismissed with a wave of the Wardens hand. So be it, we were each other's whore.

With my execution date approaching, my final class with the musical program was surprisingly emotional. Over the 14 years a lot of dedicated men passed through its doors. The quality of the music had increased remarkably and more importantly the men had reached out to help other inmates. There are numerous music classes with inmates being taught how to play and read music. It took on a life of its own. I'm pretty much just a figure head there now and I'm quite happy to take a back seat to *their* passion.

A cake was made for my final class. Hugs were aplenty and I actually teared up with emotion and gratitude for their friendship, hard work and for not shanking me. It was during the cake cutting I overheard one of the guys mentioning about his cell mate hearing the nursery rhyme.

For whatever reason this sent a chill down my spine and I asked what he was talking about. It was a common folklore in Rollins-Loch–its own version of a scary story. For as long has been remembered certain prisoners claimed to hear a very faint song at night. There have been different versions of the lore. Some say it's a child's voice, some a woman's, other times it's the voices of dead prisoners or even guards killed years ago during a riot.

The song gets louder and louder each evening, but only the one inmate can hear it. The inmate starts by asking those around him, "Can you hear that?" The same question keeps coming up every night and they lash out at others because they believe someone is fucking around with them. After a couple of weeks the inmate is screaming and crying for the voice that is singing, to stop. It usually starts a big commotion on the block because other inmates are trying to sleep and since everyone knows the *curse of the nursery rhyme*, it scares a lot of inmates as well as the guards.

From what I've been able to gather they say someone hears the song about every seven to 12 years. The unlucky inmate who has heard the song goes insane or commits suicide. There is rumour of a guard hearing the song in the late 1940's. He quit the prison, but the song followed, haunting him until he put his service revolver in his mouth to end the madness.

Gary Newport, a horn player in the music program told us all that his cell mate Cole Ortiz had heard the nursery rhyme and started a slow decent into madness. Every night he could hear Ortiz crying into his pillow begging through broken prayers for it to stop. During the days Ortiz walked around in a haze, muttering to himself, sometimes breaking into tears. Other inmates avoided Ortiz like the plague.

I'm not sure why I needed to know, but I asked Gary to see if he could get Ortiz to tell him what was being said in the rhyme and its melody. Gary and Cole are the only two inmates I mention in this story by name. The only reason I mention them is because they're dead.

Father Humber, the prison's minister has been dropping in more and more frequently since my execution date is close. He asks me if I would like to confess and ask forgiveness for my sins and to save my immortal soul. He always looks disappointed when I reject his offer. It's the same look a dog has when you go to the front door, putting on your jacket and shoes and they realize they are not coming with you when the door is slowly closed in front of them.

It was Father Humber who mentioned the deaths. He didn't have much detail other than Ortiz stabbed Gary during an altercation and then took his own life. I pressed him with questions, but the Father had no answers for me. I imagine it was Gary pressing for details about the nursery rhyme that set Ortiz off. He was slowly going mad and being pressed about it sent him over the edge.

I sat in my cell more shaken and guilt ridden about Gary's death than any of the crimes I committed. I know that if I didn't ask him to find out details about the rhyme, he would still be alive. I think Ortiz would have killed himself eventually; although I never saw him personally, it just sounded like he was a powder keg ready to go off.

I mentioned my guilt to Father Humber and he was pleased. I guess it gave him some purpose in this shit hole; so, I figure I was just helping a brother out. He told me that every prison has its ghost stories and the tale of the nursery rhyme that drives inmates mad was Rollins-Loch's version of many different stories across an imprisoned nation.

When I asked him if he felt the cold, dark, evil feeling to this place his eyes–I don't even know how to describe it. They didn't move, but I could see movement in them. I'm probably not making sense, but I could see something in them. It might have been acknowledgement or perhaps fear, but I knew at that moment he felt something in this place too. He associated my sensing of evil in this place as feelings of guilt due to the lives I had taken.

I changed the topic and he gladly went along with me. I asked him to visit me on my last day on this mortal plain to deliver this confession. I told him that I would like to keep it private and for him not to read it. I requested that it be delivered to someone on the outside and it would be published for the world to see. I promised that I wouldn't go into detail about the deaths I committed.

Father Humber promised me he would not read my confession and would pass it along to my person on the outside. He was my only hope for this to get out because I no longer had any contact with fellow inmates. I couldn't give it to the guards because I know they would have read it and destroyed it right away after reading the part about them smuggling out my music.

As of this writing, all my works written in here have been delivered to my people on the outside. There is no original work left in my cell, but I will be leaving some 'pieces' behind. I image when I am dead, and my head is still smoldering from the current that had passed through it, there will be plenty of 'scavengers' looking though my cell for one last great piece–my final work. I imagine Warden Garrison will be one of the first to run his grubby little hands in the musical pages I have left behind.

I truly hope he enjoys them, they are all untitled, but familiar. They are all sheet music to the opening themes of popular TV shows. I imagine it won't be worth much except for the odd collector who appreciates a good joke.

I go into my final night of sleep wondering if it was all worth it? Was it worth all the people I hurt in my life due to my actions? Frankly yes. All the people who have died for my music will never achieve anything close to the success I have achieved. The gift that I have given to humanity. All of them combined couldn't match what I have produced and gifted future generations.

If there is a Hell I am sure I am going there. I only just need to reread the paragraph above to know that.

If God is listening, I just want a quiet death. My fear is that when I don the hood, that I will hear a whispered nursery rhyme, or see a paralyzed boy in a wheel chair looking at me yelling "I hate you!"

Instead I hope and pray to whatever God is willing to listen, that when the hood is placed over my head, that I see a soft blue light. The same blue light that came from the radio I used to listen to in my bedroom closet as a child. I will feel warm in its glow and when I hear the beautiful music coming from its speakers, I will smile because the music I will hear will be mine.

Alexander Harlan

Ghost of La Belle

I couldn't move. Everything was dark and all I could hear was moaning from a distant voice that I couldn't make out. My entire body was throbbing. It wasn't a full-on pain, it felt more like a fire that was just covered in brush–ready to burst forth at any minute. Something was holding me down. I felt a pressure on my chest and shoulders, and I couldn't raise my hands to fend off my attacker. I started to panic, and the voice started to get a little louder, but I couldn't make out any words. My mind felt drunk, but a realization hit home with sobering clarity–I was on the battlefield and I had been hit.

My body was too weak to fight back and when I stopped my struggling, the pressure relaxed. I tried to open my eyes, but it was too bright, and I didn't hear any guns or explosions. The voice that was talking to me was a woman's. I still couldn't make out the words, something was definitely wrong with me. I must be in a medical tent away from the front line. I tried to talk but my throat was raw and my mouth as dry as a bucket of sand. Finally, I was able to make out what the woman was saying, "Would you like a sip of water?"

Since I couldn't answer I just gave a little nod. "I'll give you a little bit right now and a little bit more in a couple of minutes," said the woman. She spoke English but with a heavy French accent. "You've just came out of surgery. Some people feel sick to their belly when they wake up from it, and I don't want you throwing the water back up. I know you're thirsty, we just have to go slowly with the water."

Surgery?

The woman who was obviously a nurse, softly touched my arm. "I'm going to undo the straps on your wrists. Many people wake up confused and sometimes thrash. I didn't want you to risk hurting yourself."

That explained some things I still had no idea what had happened to me. Obviously, it wasn't good; but at least it partly explained my cloudy head and why my body felt like it was throbbing. I didn't want to think about how the pain would feel when the anesthesia wore off. The last thing I remember was taking another small sip of water then drifting off into a blackened sleep.

◊

Over the next couple of days, I was in and out of consciousness. The pillow I had my head on was damp with sweat and the sheets clung to my body. The pain was terrible. My stomach felt like it was on fire and my legs just throbbed in pain. I was in a hospital–a real one, not a tent with beds. Although my head was clearer, I had no memory of how I ended up here. I knew I was in bad shape, real bad. All I wanted to do was rest, but I was worried that I would die in my sleep. Maybe by staying awake I could fight off death.

People came in and out of my room. I would feel them poking at me and examining my injuries. I tried to lay still and let them do their job, but I couldn't help but scream out in pain when they were changing the dressing on my wounds. Mercifully I would pass out and come to after they were finished. On one occasion the nurse came in with an older gentleman. He didn't introduce himself or give me a smile. He moved my blankets and inspected the dressings, then lifted them up to see how well I was healing.

I hadn't been able to see myself. I could feel both my legs heavily wrapped and my stomach was bandaged. Thankfully my penis and testicles were not harmed. That was one of the first things I checked; I'm *not* embarrassed to admit. I had some dressing on my chest, face and around my head. My mind tried to search for what the hell happened to me. The man finished his examination and turned to the nurse and said something in French. He looked down at me and started to talk, the nurse beside him started to translate.

"Do you know where you are?" the nurse asked.

"No."

"You are in a hospital in Rouen. You were injured two weeks ago and were very seriously hurt. The first doctors that treated you said you died on the table, but they were able to bring you back. You were transferred to a British Stationary hospital still in critical condition. Doctors there did everything they could to stop the internal bleeding and to save your legs."

A chill went down my back. *Died on the table. Internal bleeding. Save your legs.* I knew I was in bad shape, but...this? I also couldn't believe it: two weeks, more time for which I had no memory of.

The nurse continued, "You had other shrapnel wounds, but it was your stomach and your legs that were the concern. Your stomach seems to be healing well. The surgeries have stopped all the bleeding and we believe you are on your way to recovery. Your legs though are another issue. We will monitor them daily and assess the situation. You are very lucky to be alive young man."

And like that he turned and walked away. The nurse looked down at me, gave a small smile and followed the doctor out of the room. *Lucky to be alive.* The words rang in my head and my legs reminded me of their trauma and started to throb and burn. Sleep did not come easy.

◊

I awoke sometime in the middle of the night positive I was back at the front lines. It wasn't because of a noise, but a smell. The sleepy confusion cleared from my head, but I could still smell something. With hesitation I lifted the sheets and took deep sniff. Yep. There was no doubt about it. At the front it was a smell that was common and a smell that is very distinct –the smell of rotting flesh. I started to yell out for a nurse.

I kept yelling and was surprised to hear yelling back at me. Unbeknownst to me I had roommates and they were less than happy to be woken in the middle of the night by one of their roommates. Not caring I continued yelling until a couple of nurses came rushing into the room. When things quieted down, I pulled the cover completely off myself and pointed down towards my legs, where I suspected–and prayed for the smell to be coming from. If the smell was coming from my stomach–well that wouldn't be good.

The nurses stepped forward and I could tell from their eyes the moment they smelled it. One nurse stayed in the room to examine my leg while the other rushed off to fetch the doctor. After a quick examination I was rushed into an operating room and was knocked out. When I woke, up I no longer had my left leg. It had been removed from the waist down.

◊

The nurse who tended to me was named Sophia. She would make small chat with me when she came into the room to change my dressings. By this point I was alone in the room. My other roommates had either died or were transferred. Nobody else in the ward seemed to speak English, but I had my doubts. I could tell from their eyes that they too had seen a lot. They might not be in the trenches, going over the top wondering if it was going to be your last day on Earth. But they had seen the aftermath. They saw a lot of young men come into their once quiet hospital and die before their eyes. Limbs blown off and so much blood. It was all in their eyes.

"You must be excited to go home," Sophia said while closely examining my remaining leg.

It hit me like a thunderbolt. I never even considered that I would be going home. The war was over for me! But what was I going home to? What kind of life was a one-legged man going to have? I know I should have been grateful to be alive, and I was, but what was in store? I was going to be a spectacle for the rest of my life. Little kids pointing, adults whispering behind my back. Maybe someone would hire me because they felt sorry for a cripple. What woman would want a broken man? Maybe I should have died on the operating table. Maybe part of my spirit did.

"How is your memory?" asked Sophia as she poured me a drink of water.

"Things are slowly starting to come back," I admitted. I still didn't remember being hit and the time leading up to waking up in this hospital. I tried to force my memory to recall what happened, and a little voice in the back of my mind said, "Be careful what you wish for!"

Fear not little voice, I couldn't remember. And really how much did it matter anyway? The memory of my injury wasn't going to fix me and would probably only give me nightmares for the rest of my life. Besides, I had enough nightmares to deal with every night.

The French have a term called déjà vu. It simply means a feeling of familiarity. Well, I had that feeling. Once again, I was woken up in the night certain I was in the trenches. Like before, it wasn't a sound but a smell. And like before I called for the nurses and was rushed into the operating room. The only difference this time was I awoke from the anesthesia with my right leg amputated below the knee. Déjà vu sucks.

I awoke one morning with my sheets and pillow soaking wet. I didn't have a fever or have an accident in my sleep, but a nightmare. A new nightmare. That little voice in the back of my mind was right, I should be careful what I wish for. Because I remember now. I remember climbing out of the trench, I remember the explosion and I remember his eyes. I remember.

◊

Sophia came in while I was staring up at the ceiling. There wasn't anything else to look at. The room didn't have a window and all the walls were painted white with nothing on them except for a little crucifix above each bed. The loneliness was worse than the pain at times. There was still a phantom throbbing coming from where my legs used to be and there was nothing around to distract myself. The hospital was very mechanical, I would get fed at the same time and someone would come with a bed pan at the same time. Nurses would come in and out to check on things, but only Sophia could understand me. I continually tried to have her sit down and talk, but she always said she was extremely busy.

I'm sure she was. If the fighting at other areas in France were as bad as the area I was in, I'm sure a lot of hospitals were extremely busy. It was madness.

"Sophia, I remember now. My memory– it's back."

"That's excellent news! I'll mention that to the doctor when I see him."

"Will you please sit down and talk with me?"

"I wish I could, but I am very busy."

"C'mon let me tell you a story about the front and what happened to me," I said trying to give her my sweetest smile. Even pouring on the charm Sophia was not interested, she barely gave a grin.

"You can tell the doctor. I have heard plenty of terrible stories from plenty of other men who were here before you. I'm sure I've heard them all."

I gave her a little shrug and raised my hands palms up as though I was defeated. There was nothing more I could say to make her sit down beside me and hear my story. I just asked her one more question and rested my head deep into the pillow with a small grin on my face.

Sophia looked at me with distrust at first, but I could see the inquisitiveness in her eyes. She looked over at the door than at the empty chair that sat by itsclf in the corner of the room. I could almost see the back and forth battle she was having in her mind, but I knew my question was too good to pass up. Sophia looked at me with a little glare and all I could do was give a genuine smile in return. She walked across the room and put the chair next to my bed and sat down. I had her full intention.

It was an easy choice for her to sit down and listen. After all, it's not every day someone asks you, "Do you want to hear a real ghost story?"

◊

I was a 15-year-old kid living outside of Toronto during the summer of 1914 and my life was a little slice of heaven. My friends and I spent countless hours down at the lake, swimming the days away and walking back home when the sky would start to turn a stunning orangey-red. I hadn't thought much about what I wanted to do with my life, and I spent less time focused on world affairs until that year.

When the war was announced that summer, I was the most excited person around–possibly the second most excited person besides my father. My parents were born in England; mom came to Canada when she was 4 and my father when he was 23. We were loyal to the King; we even had a picture of King George V in our house.

I think dad would have enlisted the day Britain declared war on Germany, but he couldn't serve his country. Dad was born with a birth defect, cursing him with a deformed right hand. He had a perfectly fine working left hand, and he could shoot a gun with it, but the argument fell on deaf ears and he was ineligible. But his dream could still be lived through me.

I was all for it. I couldn't wait for the fighting, excitement and the glory. I couldn't wait to enlist to bring honour to Britain and Canada as well as for my mother and father.

Now there was a problem with me being 15. The youngest age you can enlist was 18. My father took me down to the recruitment officer and told the recruiters that I was 18 years-old. I was a tall kid for my age, with a bit of soft facial hair. I was worried that they were going to turn us away, but they barely gave me a second glance. They did a medical check on me, and I was in the army.

I think they knew I wasn't 18, but I don't believe they cared. They were just looking at it from a numbers game. They had a quota to fill. If we were willing to fight, and didn't look ridiculously young, we were accepted.

To my dismay we didn't leave by train to Halifax until November. I wanted to be there yesterday, but there was too much foot dragging for my liking. From there we boarded a ship that would take us to Liverpool, and we were taken to our training grounds in Wiltshire. We had basic training which took six to eight weeks. Me and the other guys who signed up were all in fear that the war would be over by the time we arrived.

During our training, we'd tell any of the men that were being shipped over to Europe before us, to save some for us, and we would see them soon. How little we knew.

When we first set foot on the European mainland, it was a cold, rainy early spring day. I used to love the rain. Now, I hate the rain, I curse at it under my breath. We were piled onto a train and were dropped far from the action. It was a two-day march to the front.

We were on a road south of a place called Artois in France. We marched and sang knowing we were getting closer to battle. From a distance we could hear explosions. It got quiet among us, and then we cheered. We cheered that the Huns were taking a beating and they'd better look out because we were coming. It never occurred to us, that it might have been our side that was being blasted.

Within 10 miles of the front we got a lot quieter. The land was marked with craters and scars of war. And the smell. The smell of death. You never get used to it really. You might cope to the point where you're not throwing up all the time, but you never get truly accustomed to it. The death we smelled was from farm animals. Dead cows and horses could be seen rotting in ditches along the road and on the battered fields.

As the light began to fade, we met some soldiers walking towards us coming from the direction of the front. We gave them a cheer, but we quickly stopped when one of the soldiers in the line told us to shut the fuck up. I think we would have stopped cheering on our own after we started looking at the faces of these men.

These soldiers were only a few years older than me, had a look to them. Their faces held no smiles, but it was their eyes that scared me. They all looked the same, dark and empty. I don't know what had happened to them, but something had changed them. I looked away, obviously these men were weak, because when I'd finally get up there, I was going to almost win the war single handed with the number of Huns I planned on shooting. If it was me walking back from the front, I would be leading the men in song, cheering on others walking into battle, jealous that it wasn't me going back to kill more Germans.

With the darkness came the flashes of light. At first, I thought it must have been distant lighting and thunder, but looking directly above and seeing newly appearing stars, I realized it was distant explosions we were seeing and hearing.

The incredible part was, there was no break in it. The closer we got the louder it got, how the hell can we fight in that I thought. But the shelling never stopped, nor slowed down. About a mile from the action we were told to stop. We would continue to the front in the morning.

I don't think I slept a wink that night. I'm not sure any of us did. Laying my head on the ground, sleep a distant promise, I could feel the earth shaking from the explosions in the distance.

The next day we advanced to our new home when the shelling stopped. There were fears the Huns were going to attack, but nothing came. Except for more shells. It lasted for 2-hours then it was our time to shell them. Word came down the line that we were going to go over the top.

Beside me was Gordon Hawking, a friend I had made during training at Wiltshire. Back then we were eager to show our worth and to become war heroes. But now, waiting our turn to climb out of the trench and attack...well, I only hope my eyes didn't show the same amount of fear that was in Gordon's.

Captain Downing who had overseen our training, yelled for us to get ready. In an instant it was quiet except for a whistling sound in my ears. It was soon to be replaced with another as Captain Downing blew his whistle and we all jumped up and climbed out of our trench.

I always imagined that my first taste of war would be intoxicating. In all truth, it was a blur. I felt slow, and everything around me was moving too fast. The legs under me didn't feel like my own, yet somehow, I managed to stay on my feet.

Then as if woken from a dream, everything became clear. I heard the bullets zipping past me and the cries and screams of men wounded and dying. I tripped over something and hit the ground hard. I turned around and saw a dead soldier partially covered in dirt. I couldn't see any blood; the earth probably swallowed it. But I did notice the soldier was missing his head.

I vomited and wondered what the hell I had gotten myself into. I imagined my old classmates back home finishing up school or working. Maybe they had fallen in love and were walking hand and hand, trying to steal as many kisses as they could. None of them I'm sure were tripping over decapitated bodies while bullets were ripping apart the men around you.

I heard the whistle and calls for retreat, and I clawed and stumbled back to our trench. I found Gordon, knowing each other were still alive, we hugged and patted each other on the back. Not the same could be said for Captain Downing. He was found dead in the trench, in the exact spot I saw him before I went over. As soon as his head appeared over the trench, a bullet was there to greet him.

◊

During my first week in the trench I heard some men talking about seeing the priest. The gossip worked its way down the line. I was born Catholic, but rarely went to confession. The poor priest was going to be busy that night by the sounds of it. Sobbing men, asking if they would go to Hell because they committed one of the deadly sins thou shall not kill. Fortunately, man had found a loophole in that commandment when it came to war.

We discovered we were battling in the middle of a village. Of course, none of the people or buildings existed any more. The residents had fled, and the buildings had been flattened. The village didn't exist on any of our maps, but we had been able to find parts of a sign. The sign had been blown apart and the only letters we could on broken pieces of wood was LA and ELL.

Wanting to forget the horrors I saw now around me, I tried to picture the most beautiful place I could think of and try to give it a sweet-sounding name. I named the village La Belle. The men around me smiled, all agreeing it was the perfect name. I think it was only a couple weeks later, after steady shelling and more of our friend's dead, the place was rechristened "La Hell". I was never able to capture the beautiful image of the village again, and I was never able to get the name La Hell out of my mind.

Nervous, on edge, we thought things in La Hell couldn't get worse, and of course we were wrong. It started to rain on May 3rd, and it didn't stop for eight days. Not exactly Noah dealing with 40 days and 40 nights, but Noah wasn't bogged down in the mud with bullets whizzing by his head and shells exploding all around him.

Staying dry was a pain but trying to navigate no-man's land in the mud was worse. The goal when you go over the top is to sprint towards the Huns; avoid getting shot and get to their trench as fast as you can. When you get to their trench two things usually happened. They would retreat and counter attack–usually regaining their trench. It was a back and forth affair. They would attack and push us back, we would attack and push them back. No substantial beak through ever happened.

The scary thing when you're running in the mud, is it almost feels like time is standing still. It's like a bad dream when you try to run, but your legs just won't work. Imagine that feeling, but being shot at, and having men dying around you. What's worse is the puddles in no-man's land had a greasy appearance to it. When I asked Gordon what it was, he matter-of-factly told me it was from decaying bodies.

I nodded, knowing I should have known better. The place stank of death mixed in with vomit, urine and feces. We had toilets–a bench with a small trench dug out behind it which we used, but sometimes when a man gets pinned down, and can't move for hours, sometimes nature's calling happens right there and then.

Back in our trench, cleaning my weapon I heard mention of the priest again and how the weather doesn't stop him from making his rounds. I looked around and didn't see any priests. I figured he was talking with some of the men, and that I would probably meet him soon. When I finished cleaning my rifle and smoked a couple of cigarettes, I had totally forgotten about the priest meeting the men. Again, I looked down the trench and didn't see any sign of a priest. I figured he was held up and would come back the following day.

◊

It's crazy how people can get used to certain conditions. You learn to live with the sounds of bullets picking off people around you and the explosion of shells. When the shelling got really bad we would gather in an underground bunker, praying a shell didn't land directly above us, burying us all alive. I saw men lose their minds in there. A young soldier clawing for the doors, having to be restrained yelling they needed to get out. The cramped conditions did play with a man's mind. The smell was sickening, you could smell the fear even though everyone put on a brave face.

Like the man clawing at the door, I too could feel myself losing control. The vibration from the shells, the echoing of the explosions and the dirt falling from between planks that lined the insides of our trench and onto our heads. The constant pounding of the earth would vibrate through us, sometimes so intense I thought our insides would be turned to mush. At times like these I would just rest my hand on the butt of my pistol. It brought a morbid calmness to me knowing that if things got too bad, and I couldn't handle any more of this, I could just pull out my gun and shoot myself in the head. I always pictured myself meeting God in Heaven and when I told him why I took my own life, he would put his hand on my shoulder and say he understood.

At times we would be in the bunker for a couple of hours sometimes a couple of days. But there was no relief when the silence came. That was when we had to rush out anticipating a German attack. Sometimes they attacked. Sometimes we fought them off. Sometimes we had to retreat. Sometimes... well, nothing happened.

Near the end of summer, we even had a cease fire. Well, not an actual cease fire, but a lull in the action. I think it was both sides trying to figure things out, thinking of new ways of killing each other. Even the snipers were taking a break in the action, but we would keep our heads down, not stupid enough to tempt fate.

Gordon and I were hunkered down, enjoying a beautiful August day. Well, as beautiful as La Hell could be. We had a lot of new faces around us. I couldn't tell you how many of the men we had lost since the beginning of our war. I was friendly with the new arrivals, but I wouldn't allow myself to get too close. I refused to let myself get close to a man who I figured would probably die soon enough.

I was sitting with my face up, basking in the sun. I was smoking a cigarette, something I did with much more frequency. Gordon was beside me, slowly eating a piece of chocolate, savouring every little nibble. In our rations we were issue bread, tea and cheese along with something that resembled meat. Occasionally we would get some rum which always improved morale. We were also given tobacco which was coveted like gold and chocolate.

I hate chocolate. I couldn't stand the smell and taste of it, and even looking at it gave me a sour feeling in my stomach. Gordon on the other hand, had a sweet tooth the size of a truck. The man could live on chocolate for a year, and never get sick of it. He wasn't a smoker so he would trade his tobacco for my chocolate. It was a deal that pleased us both.

I took a drag and asked him if he had seen the priest yet. I wasn't even looking at him when I asked, just looking up at the clouds looking for any hidden shapes, just like I did when I was a small boy thousands of miles from here.

I didn't think he heard me, so I asked him again if he had seen the priest. When I didn't hear a reply, I looked away from the clouds to see what he was doing. He was staring at me. His face was pale, and he had a strange look in his eyes. "You haven't heard about the priest?" he asked incredulously.

I think he was genuinely surprised I had no idea. The priest wasn't one of our priests who held services and talked to the men. This was the priest of no man's land—the priest of La Belle. A ghost. I tried to debunk him and say it was nonsense, but Gordon would have none of it. He told me that he had seen the priest himself. He would walk from dead man to dead man, standing over them with his head bowed down.

Others claimed they saw him making the sign of the cross, but Gordon said when he saw him, his hands were folded in front. The priest ghost of La Belle had been seen first thing in the morning and at dusk, never it seems though the middle of the day.

I gave a skeptical look and Gordon promised on the life of his Gran that he was telling the truth. I reluctantly believed in him, or at least believed that he believed. Gordon loved his Gran; he talked about her often, always with a soft smile on his face. He would never lie about something on her life.

It was thought that the priest ghost brought peace to the dying and guided the spirits of the dead. Gordon saw the priest walking early one morning, then after a couple of steps the priest just faded away. He said he was lucky a sniper didn't pick him off, because his head was exposed over the trench sandbags, staring at amazement and he lingered there after the apparition left. He told me it brought comfort to some of the men, but to him it scared him to the core. More than any bullet shot at him or any shells dropped by Fritz.

I felt rather foolish that I had not heard about the ghost earlier. I wondered what I must have been doing during those times. I considered myself a good soldier, fair at worst. How could I possibly have missed something like a ghost priest?

◊

As the war plodded on, so did we. Both sides took turns going over the top and when it was done, stretcher bearers on both sides would go out and collect the injured, trying their best to avoid barbed wire and praying no undetonated shells went off next to them. The summer months soon passed, and the cold weather hit us quick and hard. I'm not sure what a typical French fall should be, but to me it was a couple of weeks of fair weather and then winter.

The winds were nasty cold and biting. Our coats we too thin and our boots were worse. All around the trenches you would hear feet stomping as men tried to get blood to them and keep them warm. Frost bite would eat a man's toes. I heard of a soldier intentionally exposing his feet to the cold and he eventually had to have toes amputated. He did it so he didn't have to fight, figuring they would send him home. Maybe at the start of the war, that might have worked, but we were too valuable on the battlefield to be sent home over a few toes.

The toeless man was sent back to the front and ended up dying in battle. It seemed only death would get us out of this war.

As Christmas approached our officers made it very clear there would be no fraternization with the enemy. Last year men on both sides of the trenches, made their way across no man's land on Christmas day. Even though many on each side had no idea what was being said, men hugged, sang Christmas carols and even played soccer. Not a single gun was fired. This year, just to make it clear, we were told if any man made any attempt to repeat the incident, they would be shot on site.

It was a few days after Christmas that I finally saw the priest of La Belle. It was the Huns who spotted him first. We heard a commotion from the German's and one of us was brave enough to peak over the top–we weren't sure if they were just trying to lure us for their snippers. Our guy, I'm not exactly sure what his name was, maybe Donald or something like that, anyways we heard him say it was him, and we all jumped to our feet and poked our heads foolishly out of the bunker.

Any fear of a snipper's bullet left me as soon as I saw the priest. He wore long robes, they were dark in colour, and it was impossible to make out any distinct features in him. But like Gordon had told me, he walked from corpse to corpse, both ours and German alike and would stand above them, head down in what appeared to be a prayer. I saw his hand slightly move up, perhaps doing a slight version of the cross. He walked a few steps more then suddenly he disappeared.

I stood watching in awe, until I remembered my surroundings and quickly got back down. It was eerie and a little bit scary seeing this spectre; but it also brought on a strange feeling of peacefulness knowing someone cared for us, even if they were from the netherworld.

◊

Life in La Hell was one miserable day after another. The men loved to gossip like little school girls. I heard stories of how the war would be over by the spring because the Germans were losing in the east, and they would collapse soon. I heard of our side having a secret weapon, I also heard of their side of having a secret weapon. Murmurings of those evil bastards using some sort of gas weapon which would burn a man's lung and make him tear at his body until he was dead. Rumours of men lying in a bloody mess, drowned from their lungs full of blood. Our fears increased when we received our gas masks.

They were bulky and hard to put on. We trained every day putting them on, at a moment's notice just in case we saw a brown fog rolling towards us. It was rumoured it had a garlicy smell to it. I'm not sure if that was true, or soldiers just making stuff up. I hated the mask. I could never get it on correctly, always leaving a small gap either on the side of my face or under my chin. The officers would yell and berate me; telling me I would be dead if it was a real situation and not just a test.

We had been living in the trenches for nearly a year and winter refused to give way to spring. One early March morning we received heavy bombardment for a couple of hours. I thought for sure both sides would eventually run out of shells. La Hell was pocked with craters and the smell of death would never leave the air. It seeped into your clothing and memory.

As soon as the last shell fell, the German's were nearly on us. It was a tactic used by both sides. Men would run across no man's land and as the last of the shells fell, we would run through the smoke and catch the enemy still under cover. It was a great plan on paper, but the execution of the strategy didn't always work. A couple of times running across no man's land I had to jump for cover when our shells continued to rain down.

On one such attack we lost 13 men to friendly fire. 13 men who would never see their families again. Men who never have a chance to see another summer–to fall in love–to have children and grandchildren. Their families would never get a chance to bury them–they were buried in the frozen mud of La Hell. But what were 13 men when the total number of dead since the beginning of the war was in the hundreds of thousands.

On this morning we came out of our shelters expecting the advance and we gave them hell. Some made it into our trenches but would never make it out again. We were battle hardened soldiers, the best in the world. We now stared down death and we fought those bastards back hard, and when we heard their retreat, we poured out of our trenches and counter attacked with bloodlust.

Upon seeing our counter attack, the Huns started shelling again, not caring that some of their own would be killed. By now we weren't men, only statistics. One of the shells landed to the left of me; it was about 20 feet away, but the explosion sent a mass of frozen mud towards me and caught me high on the shoulder. It knocked me off my feet and into a large crater.

It's amazing how quickly the mind works. I had barely landed, when I immediately did a quick inventory on my body. I reached over and felt my sore arm, it was still there, and I quickly scanned for blood. Nothing that I could see. I started bouncing my legs making sure they were still attached and reached down and felt them–just to double check. I let out a small sigh of relief that I wasn't badly injured as far as I could tell, but I knew I would be sore the following day.

It took me a few seconds to realize that I was not alone in the crater. Out of the corner of the eye I saw a German soldier sitting on the other side of the crater. My rifle was lying at my feet, so I reached for my side arm, drew and shot him three times.

I winced at the sound of the shots. In the bottom of shell hole, the gunshots echoed loudly off the surrounding earth. The German never shot back. I had shot him in the belly, but that wasn't the reason why he never fired back. Half of his head was missing, with only his bottom jaw remaining. It almost looked like an insane smile of some horrible creature.

It felt good shooting the corpse. I had such a hatred for the Germans; they had killed so many of us. The only face I recognized from all the men I had met at basic training was Gordon's because the rest of them were dead. We each knew we were living on borrowed time. The war was never going to end. We were going to be fighting until we died, and the war would only end when one or both sides ran out of men to send.

I hadn't killed any German's as far as I knew. I had definitely shot a few, but after the charges and retreats, when things quieted down, the place where the German I shot should be laying was always empty. They had either crawled back or had a buddy drag them to safety. I hope they died on the stretcher or hospital bed. It was one less man shooting back at me. Wishing for my enemy's death never gave me problems sleeping at night.

I thought I heard the retreat call, but I couldn't see or hear things clearly. The shelling had increased on both sides, and the ground shook with every explosion. Being in the middle of no man's land made it a little bit safer for me since a lot of the shells were targeted for each other's trenches. But more than a fair share fell short and would land close to me, bringing cold earth raining down. I just hunkered down, tried to keep warm and prayed a shell wouldn't land in my crater.

It started to snow softly, and I muttered a swear. The dead German across from me must have thought it was funny because he still had that big half smile on his face. I checked out his boots and noticed they were even rattier than mine and probably a couple of sizes too small. I hugged myself and just slowly rocked, waiting for the shelling to stop and thinking if I was back home at this moment, I probably would have enjoyed looking out my bedroom window seeing the soft snow fluttering down and smelling dinner being cooked in the kitchen below.

After a couple of hours the shelling never slowed, and I figured I was going to be stuck here for a while. I crawled over to my German roommate and started to take his coat off, so I could use it for a blanket. Stripping a half-headed man would have made me violently ill a year ago, but again, it's amazing what a person can endure and get used to.

I pulled the jacket free and the body shifted to its left slightly, almost falling over. I noticed a crucifix that must have been stuck in his collar, fall down, and hung freely from his neck. The skeletal smile seemed to grow on the dead soldier. In my mind I could hear him saying that we were both fighting for the same God. How was God going to decide which of his children he should support?

I wrapped myself with the coat and just tried focus on anything but the dead man across from me. As hard as I tried my eye kept drifting back to him and focusing on the crucifix. Heading into war I thought the German's were just godless creatures. They raped innocent nuns and killed new born babies in their cribs. I could see now, that at least one of them dead across from me, wasn't godless.

The waiting was worse than the cold for me. Waiting for death with each explosion, waiting for a chance to sneak my way back to our trenches. My mind whispered–waiting for the dead soldier across from me to move. I decided to check the dead man's coat pockets for anything. Something, anything to distract my mind. In my mind the dead German would reach up for his crucifix and would try talking, but only gurgling would come from his throat.

I found a wallet in the German's coat pocket. Opening it up, I found a note that was folded over and well worn. When I opened the letter, I was disappointed that it was in German. Of course, it was in German, what did I expect? I was just wanting any kind of human contact, no matter how far removed I was. In a side pocket I pulled out a picture. It was of a young man with what appeared to be his parents.

The young man seemed to be about my age, maybe a year or two older. It was easy to tell that he was related to the man and woman standing on either side of him. The woman, probably his mother, shared his eyes. They were soft, and caring.

I looked back at the corpse. There was no way I could tell if this was the same man.

"Those are my eyes," said the corpse in my mind. "Before half of my head was blown off."

The young man and the father shared the same build, and both had a crooked smile. "Not anymore," the dead German whispered.

The man across from me, hell, just a boy like me, who was I kidding. He was once loved by his parents. He loved Jesus and probably came to fight for his country and his God just like I had done. Now someone would have to tell his parents that their son had died. Never again would they get a chance to stand with him and share a picture. They would never see his crooked smile again. He was dead in La Hell with so many other young men, whose parents will never embrace him and welcome him back home.

I carefully put the picture back and I was relieved I couldn't read what was in the letter. I didn't want to read something from his family telling him they loved him, and how proud of him they were. How when he returned, they would throw the biggest party and serve his favorite food. The letter would be just like any letter I or any of my buddies would receive. I just wanted this goddamned war to end.

The shelling finally ceased later that afternoon. The flurries never increased in strength, but it was steady throughout the day.

Me and the dead German had snow all around us, and the dead man had some accumulation on his half head. I could still see his lower teeth, no longer a crooked smile, just a very wide smile.

I whistled a few times when it quieted down, and I yelled out trying to get the attention of my squad mates. I didn't yell for too long, not wanting the German's to pinpoint my location, so I didn't get a bullet in the back of my head as soon as I crawled out. "Maybe you'll look like me," the dead man said in my head.

Someone finally heard me on my side and told me to hold tight until dark. As much as I wanted to get the hell out of there, I decided I would wait until midnight to crawl out, hoping fewer snipers would be on the German side. I prayed for a cloudy night, because if the moon was out, any sniper worth his salt could spot my silhouette in the moon light and take me out.

"Don't worry," I pictured the dead soldier saying while he rubbed his crucifix, "I'm sure you'll keep your head... I almost did." He laughed with his jaw moving up and down, gurgling coming from his throat and black, thick liquid escaping from the holes in his stomach where I had shot him.

◊

Unbelievably, I must have had a quick nap because I startled myself awake. I was probably only out for an hour, but the sky had turned a dark grey as the sun was leaving the battlefield. I rubbed my legs and arms, trying to get warm when I heard something which almost made my heart stop. I sat still, head tilted waiting to confirm my fear.

I head from the German trenches, "priester." You didn't have to be a linguistic scholar to translate. The ghost priest of La Belle was walking no man's land. My heart started pounding, and my mouth became suddenly dry.

I had seen the priest of La Belle from a distance and he brought me a strange comfort knowing he was looking after the dead and guiding them to the afterlife, but that was from a distance. I didn't want to be anywhere near a ghost, regardless of it being a priest or not. I was terrified.

Suddenly both trenches were very quiet, they were watching the priest. When the priest would fade away into whatever heavenly realm he came from, there would be excited murmuring on both sides. It would be quiet for about a half an hour before shelling or shooting began, when we suddenly remembered our sole purpose was to kill our fellow man.

I curled my knees up to my chest and took very shallow breaths. I stared at my boots, refusing to look away, especially to the crucifix wearing, half headed soldier I shared this shell hole with. "He's coming for me," the German said to me in my head. His half smile bigger than ever.

I refused to acknowledge the crazy dialogue my mind was creating, and I just stared at my boots, focused only at them. Minutes past, which seemed like hours. The priest of La Belle never showed himself for very long, he must surely be leaving soon.

Then I heard footsteps approaching.

Ghosts certainly couldn't have footsteps you could hear. They were celestial, there was no mass to them. They should be walking inches above the ground, not loudly walking on it.

The footsteps started getting closer. Thankfully the dead German soldier's voice didn't appear in my mind. A thought occurred to me, what if it wasn't the ghost but maybe a German soldier. All he would have to do was look down see me curled sitting in a ball with a German coat wrapped around me and the owner of it, his brother in arms, across from me with half of his head blown off.

I ruled it out, because men never walked on no-man's land. You either ran or you died. I heard the footsteps getting closer and I just closed my eyes as tight as I could. I clinched my jaw shut, hoping it would stop any cry coming from my throat. Then the footsteps stopped.

I couldn't tell exactly how far away from me the ghost was, but I knew he was there. There were no murmurings from either trench... it was as if I could sense him near. I kept my eyes closed, feeling my bladder suddenly feeling very loose, tensing my body so I wouldn't wet myself.

Then the footsteps started to walk away. I almost pissed myself because they were a lot closer to me, than when they had stopped. But I could tell they were walking away, and then I heard the familiar murmurs of men on both sides. The priest of La Belle had left.

I didn't wait until midnight to make my escape. As soon as it was dark enough, I gave a couple of sharp whistles and waited 20 minutes before I crawled out. I left the German his coat, and neither one of us said goodbye.

As I slowly pulled myself out of the trench, I swear I could hear movement behind me. The dead German was playing possum and now he was coming for me. The smile on his half face somehow widening as his grey fingers pulling through the mud, inching his way towards me. In my mind I could see the corpse reaching out to grab my foot and pull me back down into the trench. Forcing myself to go slow and ignore the sound behind me, created from my imagination, was the closest to madness I hope I will ever experience.

Crawling slowly, I made little sounds so my men could hear me coming and know not to shoot at a strange noise. I figured it took me a couple of hours to make it back. I took no chances and went *very* slow. I could faintly hear my cohorts encouraging me on, and I finally made it back. It was thankfully a cloudy night above the battlefield.

◊

Recovery time from my experience was a couple cups of coffee, and extra blanket and a pat on the back, because we were going over the top again the next day. Around 2 the shelling from our side started. We were told it was going to be targeted and intense. During my time in the shell hole reinforcements showed up. Instead of us being relieved they decided the best thing to do was a mass charge and hopefully bust open a gap in the German lines. We were, "the tip of spear."

I'd heard that tip of the spear bullshit line countless times from countless officers. We were just a hammer meeting the anvil. Neither side was giving in.

Shelling stopped at 8 am. It was a short shelling duration compared to others, but it was fairly isolated. It was hard to imagine any German resistance, but we had been playing this same old song and dance for so long, the last thing we expected was an easy go of it.

Now when our last shell landed, we should have been over the top charging what remained of the Huns front lines. The problem was, the officers who were to give us the command to attack were expecting the shelling to stop at 9 am, not 8. There was a lot of confusion among the officers. The best thing to have done in my opinion was to reorganize, rearm and try it again in a couple of days.

The officers concerned that their higher ups would give them hell about wasting shells and not having the *stuff* to make quick decisions. Well, after nearly 10 minutes of stammering among each other, the call was made to go over the top.

I was beside one of the reinforcements, and he was eager, just biting to get at the German's. I had recognized the excitement before, sometimes nervous energy like that can be good when it came to find some extra speed and adrenaline on the battlefield. What concerned me was his eyes. He had the look like he was going to kill every German he saw, and he was going to have a good time doing it.

That look in the eye is dangerous. You always wanted to see some fear in a man's eyes because fear can help keep you alive. You never want to see cowardice or the other end of the spectrum which was where this guy was. I asked him his name, he looked at me, gave me a little laugh and just looked up at the top of the trench waiting to burst over it.

I brushed his rudeness off, it wasn't a great time after all to make friends. I tried to quiet my mind and get ready. I have no idea how many times I had made this charge, I just know for each one, I was secretly terrified.

The call went and like a cat the new guy beside was already half way up the trench ladder. I didn't hear the shot, but I did see the spray of blood and the new guy fell back into the bunker, a new hole in his face for all his effort.

I stepped into the spot where he was shot and started to climb. I figured the gunman would have swung his attention elsewhere and didn't expect someone to come out from the same spot. When I crawled out, I felt a wisp go past me. I figured if I hadn't of moved over, that bullet would have hit me where I was supposed to climb out.

For the first time since I had been at the front, I wasn't afraid. I felt as if I was under God's divine protection and that nothing would bring harm to me. I charged ahead, knowing for certain that I would live to see tomorrow. Machine gunners opened up on us and men on both sides of me fell, but I kept going.

Perhaps unconsciously I avoided going near the shell crater I had spent all the day before in. I didn't want to see the dead German's half smile or see his crucifix again. Most likely, I didn't want to go near just in case the priest of La Belle was inside, saying a quiet prayer over the dead soldier's body.

I just prayed to whoever was listening that the shelling had cleared the barbed wire. I had seen men on both sides get tangled up in it. Most soldiers have had the unfortunate experience of having a foot tangled in the wire. The key was to relax and quickly unwrap the wire and pray you didn't get shot while doing it. If you panicked and started to thrash and pull the wire would sometimes only get tighter. The wire would strip the flesh off the bones and the tighter it wound wind around your leg, it would become a death grip. Fortunately for me on that day, the wire didn't grab hold of me.

I jumped into the German trenches just in time to see them retreating. I was going to run after them, but sanity made me stay put. It was better to secure the area, then risking my life by chasing after retreating Germans. I wouldn't be able to chase them far. They had secondary lines ready to counter attack. I'm sure a German sniper would have loved seeing me running towards their secondary lines.

As it turned out, we held the trench until nearly dinner time, when we had to retreat to our own trenches. We made sure we stole any of their supplies, and some of the men dropped their pants and left a welcome home gift for Fritz.

The whole exercise was a complete waste. We had nothing to show for it except for dead and injured soldiers. If that bloody trench was so strategic, why did we retreat at the first sign of German aggression? I was brewing over this, while smoking a cigarette when I looked around, not noticing Gordon. It's easy to get separated, and to not see someone for several hours I had proven that the day before.

When I crawled back from my time in no man's land with the half-headed German,

Gordon gave me a hug and a punch to the arm saying that he was worried sick. I had no idea how long he was gone I hadn't noticed him in the German trenches. I asked around, and I found out he was one of many that hadn't returned for rollcall. I walked up and down the trenches yelling out for him. I was answered with a few sniper bullets hitting the sandbags above my head.

I wasn't the only one keeping an eye out for him. Gordon was well loved by many in our unit. He always had incredible stories to tell us, peppered with humour that many of the guys took as complete bullshit, but they loved to hear him because Gordon was such a great story teller.

I remember one time a bunch of us were huddled in our trench, freezing cold, stamping our feet and doing whatever we could to stay warm. We had just come out from our fortified bunker which we were hunkered down for the past two days because of non-stop shelling. A lot of our nerves were on edge and morale was non-existent.

Amid our despair a rat scurried along the edge of the trench with a severed finger in its mouth, dragging it behind it. We just stared and watched the rat go by, as it eventually turned down another trench out of sight.

None of us said anything, we were pretty used to seeing the horrors of trench warfare. It was Gordon who broke the silence. "Jesus Christ! Did you guys see the size of the prick on that rat?!" The guys erupted in laughter. True genuine laughter. Something that I hadn't heard since I landed in France. With one simple morbid joke, Gordon lifted our spirits giving us strength to make it through another day.

Over the next couple of days, I called out into no-man's land which we morbidly rechristened dead-man's land, because it's only inhabited by the dead. When the call went out to go over the top, I ran with my head down, trying to see if I could spot his body—an excellent way of getting myself killed. After a week, he was officially declared dead. His body was never found, another victim of the shell churned mud of La Hell. I stayed up at night waiting to see if the priest would show up. He never did.

◊

The sorrow ate at me, but it was important to focus on my job as a soldier. Not keeping your mind on your duty was an easy way to literally lose your head. The death of Gordon was cushioned with some good news, because we were going on leave. After a full year of fighting, a full year of living in La Hell we were leaving, even if it were only for a short time. We had a week's leave and we were headed for Paris–I found out that travel to and from the La Hell didn't count, so we had a solid week in Paris.

In Le Hell we rotated positions. If we weren't at the front line, we were doing other jobs. Mostly trench repairs. Repairs to the communications trench, the supply trench and secondary lines. We were constantly filling up sandbags and stacking them. I remember one time the water in the trenches was half way up our shins. The rain just kept pouring down and the water just kept rising. It didn't help my mood when I considered the Germans were living in the same conditions as us and were probably just as miserable.

A young officer came down our trench and we were carrying our shovels after a couple hours of repairs. The young officer looked down at the water he was trudging though and barked at us, "Clear up this water!"

I immediately started to scoop up water with my shovel and toss it out of the trench. Of course, the water just poured back in. The others with me started to shovel out the water as the officer looked at us with a scowl and proceeded past us. Once he was out of sight we stopped shoveling, cursed the young prick under our breath and carried on our way.

Another duty we had was taking care of the horses. For us, that meant cleaning the shit out of their stables. Most of the men loved this job because it was further away from the front lines. I hated it. I could see the fear in the horse's eyes. These poor creatures had to live in the same horrors as we did and weren't exempt from the dangers. Horses died all the time from the shells and bullets. They could smell death in the air just like us. I'm not sure if horses have a greater sense of smell than humans—I pray for their sake they don't. Horses just don't have the ability to mask their fear like we can.

Gordon and I had talked many times about going to Paris. We talked openly and honestly about what we would do. For me, the idea of having a real dinner, on real plates sounded like heaven. To have a drink of wine and to sleep in a real bed. A lot of the men were going to visit the whore houses and get a woman. I was a virgin and I was scared at the idea of going, especially with an experienced woman. I didn't want to embarrass myself; but, even if I didn't pay for sex, just to have a soft body lie down next to me and hold me.

Poor Gordon died only days before getting away. No fancy dinners, soft bed and loose women for him.

When we marched away from the front, the sounds of death were slowly fading, we saw fresh faces marching forward. We could tell they were virgin soldiers. They were singing, and all had smiles and eager looks on their faces. When we approached, they stopped singing and just watched us as we marched by. It was strange watching these young faces, with so much enthusiasm in them suddenly solemn, because of what they saw in our faces.

Had months of war changed my appearance? I'm sure it had. I was no longer a naive boy who arrived on the shores of Europe a year ago. I was jaded now. I didn't have faith in our leaders, I didn't have faith in humanity and as much as it pained me, I had no faith in God.

When we arrived at the train station and finally boarded, we collapsed into our seats. You must remember that it had been months since we sat in anything comfortable. Soon the train was full of snoring soldiers as it headed toward some rest and relaxation.

As the train rolled into Paris, my plans had changed. I just wanted to curl up in my bed with a bottle of scotch in my hand. I would make a visit to the whore house, but I didn't want comfort, I didn't want to be held, I just wanted sex–I didn't want to die a virgin. Beside my hotel room bed, on the nightstand I kept my pistol. Maybe I would use it to end my misery, maybe I wouldn't. I just wanted to spend my week sleeping, drinking, fucking and finding a reason to go on living.

We were shown our quarters, a lot of us were housed in an old hotel the army had rented for its men. There wasn't much of a view out my window looking down at the street I could see prostitutes gathering, I would make their acquaintance later, I was in no rush. I took to the streets to find some alcohol. Even after days of marching, my feet wanted to go for a walk.

When I stopped walking, I looked up at the building my feet had taken me. I sighed... I was sad, lost and broken. I opened the doors and walked into the church.

When I entered, I felt the energy, before I saw any of the stained glass, wooden pews or the image of Jesus on the cross. I didn't see anything because I couldn't see past the tears in my eyes. When I entered the church, it felt as though Jesus greeted me with a hug, and didn't let go, and I didn't want him to. I just cried.

I cried for Gordon and his family, and the life he would never have and the dreams he would never dream. I cried for my parents, wishing I could see them one more time to hug and kiss them. I cried for myself, because I didn't know if I could go back to La Hell. I just fell to my knees and let it all out. Nobody came rushing over, apparently, I wasn't the first young soldier to do this.

I can't explain why a person thinks of certain things in certain situations. My family and Gordon left my mind, and my mind's eye went back to my hotel room and the gun that was sitting on the bedside table, waiting for my decision.

The invisible hug from Jesus got tighter and warmer. I let out a final sob and my head cleared; perhaps for the first time since I had arrived in France.

For the rest of the week I walked the streets of Paris, tried some wonderful food and drank some wonderful wine. I never visited the whores who were camped out around my hotel, and the pistol on my nightstand was never touched.

The trip back to the front gave me a lot of time to think. I was still scared, but I wasn't afraid to die. The moment in the church had changed me. My love and belief in the Lord were never stronger. I believed that Jesus had sent the priest of La Belle to us, as a reminder of his love, and that he was with us, and forgave us for our sins.

It was a month after returning to the front from Paris. I had no sense of foreboding when I woke up. It was a nice day, if those even exist on a battlefield. Both sides had been shelling for days, and we were in our fortified underground bunker waiting for it to end. No longer did I need to keep a hand on the butt of my pistol, to keep me calm in there.

We were given the call to go over the top and trying to run was near impossible. So many craters and clumps of earth made it tough going. Twisting or breaking an ankle was always a threat. But our job wasn't to complain; like good soldiers we did what we were told, and we advanced.

The Huns were late with their response. We had caught them off guard with our charge and we managed to make good distance through no man's land before any shots were fired. I had my eyes straight ahead when I caught a glimpse of something come at me on my left. I heard a thump and noticed it was a grenade and I just remember diving to my left when I heard a screaming noise.

The grenade went off and it blew me through the air when something hit me from the right. I'm not sure, but I think a shell must have landed close to my right and the force of the explosion sent me flying again. It was like an invisible game of tug-of-war. I didn't feel any pain, I just remember my arms and legs flopping freely, having no control over them.

I'm not sure how long, or how far I was tossed–it seemed long, but I do remember hitting the ground. When I hit the ground, I thought I would never get up. The force was so strong, it was like I had fallen out of a tall tree. It was when I hit the ground that my body seemed to be on fire. The burning was searing, and I could swear I could hear sizzling. Then I blacked out.

I must have been out for a while because when I woke up, the sky was darkening, and the fighting had stopped. I could only hear a slight buzzing noise, and a muffled sound like my head was submerged under water. I knew I was hurt bad. I felt the tears run down my face because I knew there was no way for me to crawl back to my trench or shelter. My body was in total pain and exhaustion overtook me.

I knew I was going to die. My body felt like it was slipping. I wish I could explain it better. My body was hurt badly, and my soul was starting to awaken, ready to make its parting. My mind went back to the church in Paris, and the warm hug I felt from Jesus. I tried to take my mind back to that time. To feel the warm hug of the Lord instead of the battered earth of France.

It was thinking of that church when I caught an image out of the side of my eye. It seemed to take a lot of effort just to turn my head and that was when I saw him–the ghost priest. There was no fear in my heart, just a little sadness. I knew he was coming to take me home, but I mourned for what my life could have been, and what I could have done. But God was calling me, and he had sent down his guide to the afterlife.

I saw him coming towards me. He stopped a couple of times, for other fallen soldiers I assumed, I couldn't see. He seemed like a real man, he seemed solid enough, but I noticed he moved very smoothly. The earth was so devastated there wasn't a flat section for miles, yet he moved effortlessly. I tried to listen for footsteps like those I heard in the crater with the dead German, but my ears were still ringing from the explosions.

As he approached, I was ready for him. I started to raise my hands toward him, so he could take me... when I suddenly stopped. I let my hand drop, and I felt my bladder release. It was the priest's eyes–they just stared coldly down at me. There was no comfort behind them, no warmth. They had anger and contempt in them, not love and peace. He wasn't an angel sent by God to bring mercy to dying soldiers.

He was more of a spirit forced in some sort of purgatory to roam the battlegrounds of men forever. He made a slight move with his hand, what I once thought was him doing the sign of the cross. Now...now I wasn't sure what he was doing, but I no longer wanted to go with the priest. I didn't want to go with him and spend the afterlife walking the grounds of La Belle.

I just screamed. It caused me pain, but that was okay. Pain meant I was still alive, so I screamed. As I closed my eyes to this entity, I thought I saw him stepping towards me. I expected to feel a cold, dead hand on my mouth to end my screams.

I have no idea of what happened after that. Stretcher bearers must have found me and carried me off. They must have heard my screams.

◊

Sophia looked at me hesitantly waiting for the story to continue, but I was done. I think the ghost story she wanted to hear wasn't the ghost story I had just told her. I wish it was a different ghost story too. The priest's eyes would always stay with me like the phantom itch coming from my missing legs. Sophia rose from her chair and poured me a drink of water.

"You will be moved to a new room tomorrow," she said totally out of nowhere, not wanting to comment on my story at all. "It will have a window so you can finally get some sunshine and I'll make sure to move the bed close to it, so you can have something to look at instead of these drab walls." She looked around the room unsure of what to do with herself and she headed for the door. "I'll drop in later to see how you are doing." And that was that. Sophia never did come back that night. Another nurse came in to check on me.

That night I was left with only my mind to keep me occupied. Many patients in my position would be glad to get a room with a window, to have something to eat into the boredom of the day. But I was afraid of what was outside the window. I didn't want to look out in the direction of Le Hell to see the priest standing outside my window beckoning me to join him. After all, I was the one that got away. Although I was eventually going to go home, part of me will always remain in a small patch of mud and dirt somewhere in eastern France—known only to a few as La Belle.

Monkey Do

This is a story about the Devil, and his name is Maurice.

◊

The Devil walked into the small brick building which housed his psychiatrist's office. Upon entering the building, he took the narrow staircase to the left, which had flaking paint on the wall, and always had a musty smell regardless of the season. He walked up the stairs to the third floor down the corridor and stopped at the third room to his right.

Inside the small waiting room was six uncomfortable chairs, with a long table in the middle that was covered with outdated magazines. Below the window—which had a view of the parking lot—was a small table with an intercom machine on it. Above it was directions on how to use it.

1. Press call button and release.
2. When you hear a loud beep, press and hold the talk button and give your name. Release button when you are finished.
3. Please take a seat and you will be called into the office.

The Devil pressed the button. When the beep arrived, he stated in a clear voice. "Hi doctor Mortenson. It's Maurice." A garbled response came from the machine and Maurice sat down.

Now the Devil didn't really need any therapy. He had no relationship problems, he enjoyed his work, and he had no mother issues. No, unlike the beliefs of many, the Devil didn't create major catastrophes or mass killings. He considered that cheating. Plus, he knew God would not allow that much carnage. Usually by turning just one person, it can set of a chain reaction of events.

He flipped through some old magazine's that were on the table in front of him, just looking at the pictures, passing time. Plenty of fashion tips and celebrity recipes in the pages but nothing that tickled his fancy. Lots of Hollywood gossip that bored him and of course the latest diet craze. Was this what God had planned for humanity when he created the universe?

The door opened and two women walked into the office. The Devil looked up from his magazine to observe them. One was a middle aged woman, heavy-set possibly in her 50's, walking with a younger woman, heavy-set as well, probably in her late 20's. It was easy to tell that it was mother and daughter, there was no mistaking the resemblance. There was also no mistaking that there was something off with the daughter. She kept her head down and her hands were twitching the entire time.

Both women were winded from taking the stairs. There was an elevator that opened up right in front of the waiting room, maybe they were taking the stairs for exercise. The older woman pushed the intercom button and announced herself to Dr. Mortenson. Again, the good doctor mumbled a response. They took a seat across from the Devil and tried to catch their breath.

Maurice had been seeing Dr. Morty for a short time. The Devil didn't have social anxiety or emotional issues, he just like interacting with humans. This is the best way for him to understand humans and to judge them. The Devil would walk into Dr. Mortenson's office and sit in the chair in front of the desk.

"Good afternoon Maurice. How are you feeling today?"

"I couldn't be better. And you?"

The doctor folded his arms on the desk. "I've been fantasizing about Samantha a lot," he said as casually as talking about the weather.

"Remind me again Morty, who's Samantha?" Maurice asked with a grin. The doctor always opened up about his hidden fantasies and desires. Maurice doesn't use this ability on everyone he meets, he likes to pick and choose. The purpose of it is not to influence people into doing something against their will. The Devil is a big proponent of free will. But in revealing their secrets to the Devil, it brings those thoughts more to the conscious mind and out of the subconscious. The dreams and fantasies seem more attainable if the person wishes to pursue them. It becomes a test of a person's morality and beliefs.

"Please call me Dr. Mortenson. Samantha is my next-door neighbour."

"Oh right. And how old is she again?"

"17," Morty replied honestly. He would be horrified to know he confided this to anyone. When Maurice's time was up, the doctor will only remember that the patient had on going mother issues and a fear of commitment.

"What are you fantasizing Morty?"

"Please call me Dr. Mortenson. The girl is gorgeous. I tell you when I was a teenage boy, girls never looked that good! There might have been one or two, but nowadays they are everywhere! Anyway, you know how some girls don't look good with short hair? Well, her pixie hairdo looks stunning on her. She's always wearing yoga pants that are just advertising her cute little ass and she has those young, perky breasts that round out any top she is wearing."

"Do you talk to her?"

"I say hi when I see her and I'll ask her about how she's doing in school sometimes," Morty truthfully admitted. "I have to almost force myself to keep eye contact with her because I don't want to get caught checking her out. I don't want to appear pervy."

"Have you ever tried flirt with her? Perhaps in a joking way to see how she responds."

Morty gave a little laugh. "No. It would be completely inappropriate for me to do that. I've thought about taking a picture of my penis and mailing it to her, but women don't get off on that sort of thing like a man would. Right now I just like to watch her from afar. A couple of weeks ago I saw her throwing a football with a girlfriend of hers. I was in the bathroom shaving and I heard them. I opened the blinds just a bit so I could peak through and I masturbated watching her in her yoga pants and t-shirt. When I finished Samantha yelled out and jumped on the other girls back trying to tackle her. Both girls were laughing on the ground fighting for the ball. It only lasted maybe a minute or two but seeing them on the ground got me excited again and I imagined a lesbian relationship between the girls. I came again in no time. I hadn't been able to do that since I was a teenager. I was rather impressed with myself."

"I'm sure you were Morty," Maurice said. "Do you think 17 is a bit too young for you?"

"Please call me Dr. Mortenson. Of course, 17 is too young but Samantha doesn't look 17! I mean she could pass for a woman in her early 20's no problem. It breaks the spell when I talk to her tough. She might look like a woman, but she still has a mind of a teenager. It ruins the fantasy."

"Any other desires?"

"Well I have a lot of women who come in here and are totally unhappy in their marriage. Some are bored and feel they want a change.

Some are in abusive relationships and want me to tell them what to do. Some have spouses cheating on them and some are cheating on their husbands. None of the women that come in here are as sexy as Samantha, but some are good looking, and you know, they have *experience* on their side if you know what I mean."

"You tell me what you mean," Maurice said wanting to draw these feelings more to the surface.

"I mean these women have sexual experience. With some of these women, they have sexual tension just ready to burst out of them. Many of them are looking for a man to listen to them, be attentive and show some affection. If a man can take care of the emotional needs for some of these women, they will take care of the man's sexual needs, and then some."

"What about you Morty? Are you the man who fits that bill? Can you give them the emotional needs?"

"Please call me Dr. Mortenson. Sure I can. I've been trained in all of that. Even if I had no intent other than purely physical, I can fake it. I know the right things to say and I can adjust to their reactions and statements. If I wanted, I could probably bed a couple of my patients."

"Are you going to make any sexual advances on the girl next door or any of your patients?"

"I think I'm content just fantasizing about Samantha. She'll be out of the house in a couple of years going to college and I won't see much of her after that. Usually when I cum and get the poison out I feel better and come to my senses. I don't want to ruin my marriage over a piece of ass – even a hot ass like hers. As far as my patients... I don't think so."

"That doesn't sound very convincing Morty. Do you think you'll make any sexual advances for one of your patients?"

"Please call me Dr. Mortenson," Morty said once again with a patient look on his face. "I can't just come out and flirt, I have to be subtle about it. I've often thought that maybe I should greet them in my office with my fly open."

"That's very subtle," said Maurice not hiding his sarcasm that Morty never picked up on.

"Yeah. I figure if she notices and looks uncomfortable or tells me I'd fake embarrassment. I'd be looking for one of the women to notice but not seemed bothered or possibly a bit excited. If I get a positive reaction I was considering when I'm sitting at my desk, that I'd pull out my penis. She wouldn't be able to see it, but it would be exciting for me. I figure after doing that for a few sessions, I might play with myself under the desk." Morty looked around the room admiring his diploma's and his collection of books on the shelves. He took his time thinking about what he was going to say, and the Devil never rushed him. "I still have the risk of losing my marriage and my practice if I get caught in an affair with a patient. But a middle-aged woman is much more discreet that a 17-year-old. If she's married she has a lot to lose too, so she'll be much more careful."

◊

As Maurice sat in the waiting room, he smiled thinking about his sessions with Morty. The Devil never told him to act out towards his neighbour's daughter or his female patients. When telling the fantasies to the Devil, it was like switching from a black and white screen to a colour screen for the person. The fantasies looked, sounded and felt more real–Maurice couldn't control that. Human senses increased when they were around him. The ultimate decision was up to Dr. Mortenson, the Devil was just enjoying the moral struggle the doctor was putting himself through. He had no idea if Morty would ever act on any of his sexual fantasies, if he were to guess there was nothing there with the neighbour other than teen lust which he could hold in check. With his patients he could maybe see him sitting with his dick out but nothing more–but the Devil had been proven wrong before with human's poor choices.

Finally getting settled into their chairs in the waiting room the older of the two women finally seemed to catch her breath and smiled at the Devil. "Hi, how are you?"

"I'm doing well thanks," Maurice said with a sweet smile on his face. "I think the doctor is running a bit late today. I was supposed to see him 10 minutes ago, so you probably have a long wait ahead of you."

"Oh, we like to come early," the mother said patting her daughter's hand. "Darlene likes coming here and is very content even if it's just sitting in the waiting room."

"It must be the comfortable chairs," he said directing the joke at Darlene.

"Darlene doesn't speak," said the mother. "I don't know if she really knows what's going on around her."

"Have you noticed any progress with the doctor?"

"Oh, the doctor isn't for her, it's for me." She said honestly with no hint of embarrassment. "I'm sorry my name is Hazel, and you are...?"

"I'm Maurice." He said reaching out shaking her hand, exchanging pleasantries.

Hazel was the type of woman who needed no coaxing when it came to sharing her life story. How her parents died when she as 17. She got married to a man not because she loved him, but because she didn't want to be alone. They were married for a year before he cheated and left her for another woman. After a series of failed relationships, she met a man she loved and got married a second time. They tried for a baby but after a series of miscarriages and gave up on the idea. A few years went by and Hazel became pregnant again. She refused to lose this one. She put herself on strict bed rest, determined to bring the baby to term. She gained a large amount of weight; her husband became very concerned for her health, but it didn't matter to Hazel. All that mattered was the baby.

There were scares along the way. But, after nine months Hazel gave birth to a baby girl and they named her Darlene. The doctors noticed early on there was something wrong with Darlene. She didn't respond to stimulus around her. At the moment none of that mattered to Hazel, she had her baby. Husband number two died in a car crash when Darlene was two. It was a devastating time in Hazel's life. She was alone again with a toddler with something wrong with her.

She admitted that things just got too much for her and she needed someone to talk to. "Darlene seems to like it too. I don't think she understands what is going on, or what is being said, even when some of it is about her. It calms me after a session and I think she feels that off me, and it relaxes her too."

The Devil decided to have a closer look into Hazel's mind and he found the one thing she would never share with him, or any doctor—a secret she planned on taking to the grave. The death of her second husband devastated her—to the point where she didn't want to live anymore. The pain of his death seemed to grow each day, and everything around her was a reminder of him. She just wanted to end the pain; end the thoughts in her head and the torment of each day without him.

But there was one thing that stopped her, her miracle baby. Her miracle baby who was now a toddler, diagnosed with severe autism. It was like she was trapped in her own little world. Every time a new toy was placed in front of Darlene there was hope for an awareness and attention towards the toy, but like most everything else in her life, she would eventually just look past it with a vacant look in her eyes. Hazel knew this little girl was the only thing that was keeping her alive, but it was like God was playing a cruel game with her. A little miracle that looked through her, rarely smiled and giggled like regular babies. The baby hardly cried, something Hazel couldn't stop doing after losing the man she loved.

She would dress her up so pretty, but it was like dressing a doll. Unless another miracle happened, her daughter would never say 'I love you' or even just 'mommy'. She would never see her daughter fall in love, see her walk down the aisle. Hazel would never get to hold her grandchildren. She could kill herself, but Darlene would be institutionalized for the rest of her life. She wouldn't know any different, but what if deep down she was aware? She couldn't risk it.

A quiet voice in the back of her head whispered to Hazel that she might be doing Darlene a favour if she ended her life too. The Devil couldn't take credit for putting that voice in her head. Humans had a darkness in each of them. It was just a matter if a person chose to go into the darkness or not.

That night Hazel prepared herself. She gathered her medications and poured them out onto the table in a small pile. There were some painkillers, antidepressants and more than enough sleeping pills. She poured herself a glass of white wine and placed it next to the pills. She went into the bathroom and started to fill up the bathtub while she went into her bedroom and into the walk-in closet. She came out with a dress that was protected in a vinyl cover. She unzipped her wedding dress.

She wanted to put the dress on, but she was too large to fit into it. She simply laid it out upon her bed and put on the vail. At least something still fit. With the white vail lowered she walked into Darlene's room and picked up her daughter. She put her on the change table and undressed her. She carried her baby into the washroom, Darlene didn't try to reach out and explore the newness that was the white vail, she just had her usual vacant eyes.

Motherly instincts still kicked in as she checked the water temperature before she lowered her baby into the water. She plunged her miracle into the water and wept. It was for the best, and when she was done, she would take her baby into her room, take the pills, and lay on the bed together and spend eternity together—a life where her husband was waiting for them and Darlene was a normal, healthy girl. She looked down into the water and the little toddler still had an expressionless look on her face. Air bubbles escaped from her nose, but she didn't flail in her mother's arms.

Darlene's dull, uninterested eyes suddenly cleared at locked eyes with Hazel. They were bright and intense, and totally aware of the moment. The clarity left her eyes as quickly as it appeared, and her eyes began to close. But it was enough for Hazel. She couldn't go to the grave knowing somewhere deep inside her daughter was cognisant of what was happening. The last image would be of her murderous mother.

She pulled her out of the tub and placed the toddler over her shoulder and started to smack her on the back. She didn't know if Darlene was breathing or not and she didn't know CPR, but she kept smacking her back hoping she would spit out any swallowed water. When Darlene started crying loudly, her lungs at first sounded watery, but soon became loud and strong. Hazel sat down against the tub and rocked her daughter as she cried too. She flushed the pills down the toilet and made a promise to herself and her little girl that she would get help.

She kept that promise. She never went longer than a year without therapy, but she would never share the details of that desperate night.

With most of her life story told—but not the entire story—the two women looked out of the window for a moment when Hazel reached for her purse and muttered, "Oh poop!"

Maurice only looked at her with eyebrows raised in a questioning manner.

"I left my cell phone in the car," followed by another "Oh poop."

She looked out the window towards the direction of the parking lot. "I better get it. It's not good to leave it in a hot car."

"Actually, it's pretty mild out today. I read a study on heat and at what temperatures they affect the phone. It would have to be another ten or twenty degrees hotter before you had to worry about it." Actually, the Devil didn't read any studies on cell phones and heat, he just knew the reason she wanted the phone was to play "Candy Crush" on it. She also figured while she was down there, she could have a cigarette too.

"Well, better safe than sorry as my granny used to say." She looked down at Darlene who was just looking out the window at nothing in particular. "I'm just going to leave her here. She won't bother you none, and she won't wander off. She'll be fine."

Hazel started walking towards the exit to the stairwell.

"There's an elevator here," Maurice said pointing to its doors. Sometimes even the Devil tried to be helpful.

"Oh, thank you but no. One time we came here and we got stuck on it. It was only for five minutes, but it felt like an hour to me. It won't do that again to me, I'll just stick to the stairs. Thank you though." The Devil just gave her a nod and looked out the window himself.

While he was lost in his thoughts, he noticed something out of the corner of his eye. It was Darlene. While he was looking out the window, he was tapping his index finger on his leg. Looking over at Darlene he noticed she was looking in his direction and was tapping her index finger onto her leg. The proximity to Maurice must have drawn her out consciously. Most people's senses were heightened around him, as was the case with Darlene.

The Devil was interested how much he could bring her out of the rabbit hole. He started slowly strolling all his fingers onto his lap and observed. The change in rhythm and fingers seemed to throw her off, but only after a few moments she was mimicking his actions.

He had a new toy, and the Devil wanted to play. He focused his entire attention to Darlene looking at her eye to eye. She was looking toward him, but her eyes were not focused onto his. He stuck out his tongue for 20 seconds and watched and waited. After a short time, a pink tongue darted out from between her lips and quickly went back in. The Devil smiled. He knew he didn't have much time left to play, he could sense that Hazel was finishing her cigarette and would be making her way back.

The Devil stretched out his arm and pulled a switch blade knife out of his back pocket. Of course the knife wasn't there when he arrived at the doctor's office: the perks of being the Devil! The blade shot out of the end with such speed it made Darlene give a slight jump in surprise. Maurice held the knife up and turned it over and over again as they both watched the fluorescent lights overhead make the sharpened steel shine bright with each turn. The Devil never looked at the knife but kept his eyes on Darlene. The tip of the knife was slowly lowered down towards his wrist. He lowered it and plunged the sharp tip into his skin and deep into his wrist. A pool of blood rose from the cut and a small moan escaped Darlene's throat. The Devil pulled the knife back towards his elbow slowly, with blood gushing out as the blade cut though tendons, muscle and veins. When the Devil finished, he placed the switch blade on the cheap Ikea table between them—blood dripping from the blade onto the table.

Maurice stood up and walked out leaving a trail of blood behind him. A trail of blood that only Darlene was able to see. The Devil left the office and into the elevator leaving Darlene with a switchblade knife and free will. It was the ultimate test of the girl's newly diagnosed obsessive compulsive behaviour. She mimicked every action he made, could she do this one? When the elevator doors closed, the Devil could still see Darlene sitting in the chair staring at the knife her hands wringing in her lap.

He could also see Hazel panting up the last few stairs taking a break to catch her break. She didn't want everyone to see her so out of breath before she opened the door and made it back to the waiting room. When the elevator pinged, announcing it had reached the lobby floor, the Devil heard a piercing scream from the floors above him. He saw Darlene slumped over in her chair with an enormous pool of blood on the floor and a massive gash running up her arm. Poor Hazel would forever wonder where her daughter had found a switch blade and why she took her own life. She wouldn't have any recollection of the nice man named Maurice sitting across from her in the waiting room, and Morty would have a blank appointment entered in his computer that was originally slated for the Devil.

◊

A month later the Devil sat down on a park bench and enjoyed the sunshine and the relaxed conditions around him. He hadn't thought of Darlene and Hazel for a long time and decided it was time for an update. He opened up his mind.

◊

The funeral was a devastating. It was tough enough to lose her miracle child in such a horrific way, but the stares from the people who came to the service seemed worse. Hazel kept her eyes down studying the carpet pattern on the funeral parlours floor. She felt certain that people were watching whispering about her and watching her body language. She hated being judged but she couldn't blame them. There was a police investigation into the death and numerous questions about how Darlene got a hold of the knife.

The police didn't believe that Hazel had murdered her daughter, but there was doubt about the knife. How did an autistic girl come into possession of such a weapon? Doctor Morty mentioned to the police that no knife was in the waiting room, but also defended Hazel saying she would never allow any harm to her daughter and he would testify to that. At the service friends would give their condolences but when they walked away, they wondered if Hazel did snap after years taking care of Darlene. Maybe she gave the knife to her daughter hoping she would kill herself.

After the funeral Hazel stayed inside not wanting anything to do with the outside world. The police said they were wrapping up their investigation and an official decision would probably be made the following week and that she should seek legal counsel–just in case.

She stayed in the following week. She wandered into the kitchen wondering what she wanted for dinner. In no mood to cook and she settled for a can of Italian Wedding soup. She heated it in the microwave and ate in front of the TV and flipped through the channels with nothing holding her interest. When her dinner was done, she rested the bowl in the sink and went to the fridge and spotted the bottle hiding in the back.

It was a bottle of Del–Gatto Estates wine and she opened the bottle and poured herself a glass of her favorite white. Hazel smiled, pleased with the taste, and went to the cupboard over the oven. She saw the pill bottle, gave it a little shake to see if there were any pills inside and placed it on the counter. She went back to her wine and finished the glass. After a quick refill she went into the bathroom and drew a bath and prepared everything. After about 10 minutes she came back into the kitchen and picked up the pill bottle. It was muscle relaxants that she had for a strained back two years ago. Hazel figured they should still be good—or at least good enough. She opened the bottle and saw 7 or 8 small pills in the bottom. She lifted the bottle and tilted the contents into her mouth and washed it down with some more wine. She refilled her glass and started to disrobe as she walked to the bathroom.

After she was naked, she reached for the light switch and turned it off; the walls seemed to be alive around her. She had six candles in the little bathroom and the light from the flames danced along the walls and the ceiling. When she drew the bath she added a lot of hot water. Hazel had read somewhere that hot baths weren't good for you. "Oh well", she thought as she dipped her toe into the water. It was hot, but after entering slowly, she acclimatized to the temperature after a short time. She was starting to feel light headed and that was okay. She took another drink and that too was okay. Hazel looked down and saw the razor blade sitting on the edge of the tub. The lights from the candles made the metal of the blade glow.

She picked up the blade and almost dropped it in the tub. That would not be okay. Her eyes were feeling very heavy. She lowered her arms under the water, and she held the blade to her wrist. She didn't cut as deep or as long as Darlene had, but she cut enough. There was pain, but the wine, pills and hot water helped lessen it. She dropped the blade and it sank to the bottom of the tub—she wouldn't be needing it anymore. She was going to see her family again. She couldn't live alone.

Hazel tilted her head back and closed her eyes. The only thing she wished she had was bubbles. She loved a good old bubble bath but she was all out, but that was okay. She felt herself drifting. The sadness was starting to leave, and she waited for the white light to appear so she could be with her husband and miracle daughter again.

◊

The Devil got up from the park bench with a smile on his face. He looked down at his watch—he had to go. Maurice was having marital issues and needed legal advice. He couldn't wait to get to know his lawyer.

14

This is a story about playing a game I never wanted to play. I never played soccer as a kid, maybe the odd time when we were in gym class but that was it. When I became an adult, to play soccer they had to make me do it kicking and screaming: literally!

Playing in the penitentiary league is a death sentence. Being in prison is bad enough, but to be forced to play this game is barbaric. I may feel that way, but I think I'm in the minority. When I step out onto the field with over 60,000 fans screaming, cheering and yelling, "you're fucking dead", I think others feel differently about the game.

Who would have thought years back that this game would be America's number one sport? It kicks the shit out of football, and all the other previously big sports. I guess not enough blood lust in those games.

I don't really want to get into my past. As far as ending up in prison it was my fault. My girlfriend and I were living in western New York and I killed her and her lover. I'm guilty, no question. Do I regret it? Every fucking day.

She was cheating on me and for my misfortune and theirs I caught them. I got mad and I lost it. I don't even remember grabbing the gun, but I certainly remember the handcuffs. The worst thing of it is: at trial I found out she was pregnant. I have no idea if it was mine or not–as if it mattered. I was devastated and wanted to die. Well the courts agreed and put me on the New York State soccer team. Number 14.

Fans will want to know why I chose the number 14? They gave it to me. I never had a choice, it wasn't my lucky number and it never meant anything to me.

When I was in the change room for my first game, I prayed for the prisons of the past. Each day waking up in a small cell, eating crappy food and always being on the lookout in the shower room. But those days are long gone. I looked around the room at my fellow inmates/teammates and I could see the fear in each and every one of them. Some were just better at hiding it than others. When I stepped out onto the pitch, I just wanted to cry and run for cover and hide. But there was no hiding for me.

All that was on the field were two nets. On the sidelines, a fenced-in bench for each team. The ramp we came up onto the field was boxed in with bulletproof glass. The playing field was also surrounded by a 35-foot seamless, bulletproof glass barrier. Between the bulletproof wall and the stands was a 20-foot buffer that was patrolled by soldiers with very large guns. I couldn't see any, but I can guarantee that there were snipers watching us very closely.

When the ref blew his whistle, the game began. The players would go for the ball, but they would always be glancing over their shoulders. I just played my position and waited.

We didn't have to wait long the roar of the crowd told us. It was always that fucking roar that told us. I glanced over to the sidelines and the game was now officially on. I fucking ran as fast as I could.

I dared to glance over my shoulder and there they were. God, I hate fucking zombies.

◊

I don't need to give you a history lesson on how it all happened. All we really knew was it started in China. The military said the Chinese were working on a biological weapon. I personally believe it was all an accident. I never trust what the military says.

But what we do know is when all of China started being over-run with fucking zombies, someone over here thought we could help out. So, they flew in some samples of the zombie blood.

Well the road to hell is paved with good intentions. Someone somewhere fucked up. Either an infected person got into the country or there was an accident with the blood samples in a lab. Before you knew it, the virus spread across the US. It is not an airborne virus like a good old fashion zombie movie you must be bit. Well, really it is just exchanging fluids, like blood and saliva. But since nobody wants to fuck a zombie, and they don't want to fuck you, they bite. I guess it is like sex for them because that is the only way they can reproduce.

Now we are not talking about rising from the dead, kind of zombie here. Zombies are alive, and when they die, they stay dead. The virus gives them an urge to attack people. They go around biting or if they are hungry or really off their rocker they will just eat the victim.

When the spread of zombies was at its worst, it was a real cluster-fuck for the whole country. That is until the military took over. It was a coup really, but no one really gave a shit because—well, because there were fucking zombies running all over the place.

The military killed the surviving leaders, and the 'powers that be' took over full control. They then went on a full offensive. They killed everything in their way, and if citizens got in the way, so be it.

Don't get me wrong. I don't trust them when they tell us things, but I sure love the fuckers for what they did. They saved our country and secured the borders. Both Mexican and Canadian borders are sealed like Tupperware. There are only designated entry points. If anyone tries to sneak over any other way, they are killed on site.

All flights have been cancelled. Only military aircraft can be in the air. They shut down commercial flights to reduce the risk of contamination. Keep the country sealed and let other countries deal with their shit and we'll deal with ours.

Global communication is not what is used to be. In the days when we had the internet, we could find out about things as they happened. Now, all we hear are rumours.

As far as I know, most world leaders have been killed and it is now a militarized world. Some countries have solved their zombie 'problem' and some are completely overrun. At least that is what I have heard.

When our country was cleaned up, our economy was the shits. There was a lot of crime, and we were on the verge of complete chaos. Well, the military stepped in again. They took over the courts and the first thing they did was get rid of the lawyers. They had three judge panels, and the people involved would plead their innocence and the judge's majority would decide their fate.

To help meet expenses, they decided to start the soccer league. They got murderers from every state and made them play soccer. The only catch is they would release two zombies. The stadiums are as tight as a drum. Soldiers everywhere, all safety requirements to the max.

If the virus were to somehow spread into the crowd, the soldiers have orders to kill on site. Of course, that is what I hear, I have no inside knowledge. Actually, we have no contact with the outside world. We are kept in our own little world. No visitations, no letters, no nothing. Just soccer.

◊

They say the first game is always the worst. I had no position to play, like full back or striker, we just went on to the pitch and played and I had no idea what to do. Not that it mattered, the crowd wasn't there to critique our play, they were there for blood.

When the roar came, so did the zombies. There are two kinds of zombies according to Hollywood. The first are the slow, dumb zombies with arms outstretched mumbling for brains. The second are scary, fast fuckers. God, I wished we had the first kind.

So, the zombies come sprinting on the pitch and players who are near them fuck off to a safer part of the field, while the rest continue to play. There is only one referee on the field, and it is his job to make sure the play continues.

The refs I heard volunteer for this gig. They have a two-foot long taser, so if a zombie goes after them, they can defend themselves. These guys are so-called adrenaline junkies, who claim they love living on the edge. I look at them as sadistic fucks who just want to be close to the horror of it all. They just want to see the gore up close and feel like big shots because they are risking their lives too, all in front of a huge crowd.

There are no linesmen, but no one really cares who kicked it out last. As long as there are zombies, the crowd is happy. The ref has the power to give out yellow and red cards like regular soccer. If teams are not making an effort to play, he can give out cards.

There are not a lot of cards given out, mainly to flagrant fouls. The refs are told beforehand to lay off the cards, only if necessary. If they give out too many cards, then they will never ref again.

In regular soccer, yellow cards are a warning, and a red card is an ejection. In my game, they have different intentions. If a player gets a yellow card, he is made to wear a 25-pound vest. A red card means the player must wear another 25-pound vest.

Being chased by zombies while being weighed down is great incentive to be a good boy and play the stupid game.

During my first game it took about 10 minutes until one of the fuckers started chasing me. And holy shit was it scary! They just make these grunting, small screaming sounds as they chase you. If they catch you and bite you, it doesn't take long for the virus to take over and you're a zombie looking for someone to bite. Hence to say there was no room for lazy or clumsy teammates.

The key is keeping your eyes open. The last thing you want with a zombie chasing you is accidentally running into the other one. I kept running and the bastard kept chasing me. Zombies can get tired, but they are like a machine when they are chasing someone. They don't know when their body gets tired and they keep trying to run at full speed. When they do tire, they sometimes collapse, and some zombies have had heart attacks on the pitch.

A lot of my teammates were swearing at me when I was being chased. Players hate nothing more a dumb ass on the team. They screamed at me to run at opposing players.

Zombies have short attention spans for some reason. They can be distracted very easily, by the crowd or other players. I ran at a guy on the Florida team and made a quick turn. When I turned around the zombie was chasing the other guy.

My lungs were burning, and my legs were spent. I thought I was in good shape, but years of smoking and a soft life had caught up with me. I fell on the turf and laid on my back trying to catch my breath. I was lucky I wasn't killed because I totally forgot about the second zombie. Thankfully for me he was at one end of the pitch banging against the bulletproof glass, not caring about the players, wanting to get at the fans.

When I heard the whistle, I thought it was half time. But it was the ref giving me a yellow card for lying down. An inmate came out with the 25-pound vest and put it on me. Now the inmate is not a volunteer in this. Usually they use life criminals or sex offenders to come out onto the field. They have no taser, and they can be and have been attacked by zombies.

I was completely knackered and now I had to run around with 25-pounds on me. And it wasn't even halftime. Obviously, I made it, but I had no sympathy from teammates. In the change room after the game no one talked to me, and for the remainder of the season I was called Shit Brains.

I made my mind up then and there; it was time to get into shape. Now mind you I didn't look out of shape. I've always been kind of skinny, but I never had any endurance.

For every practice I would just run up and down the field at full speed. Usually at the end of practice I would be throwing up. "Why don't you sprint to the toilet Shit Brains!" Such wonderful and supportive teammates. But over the years I am glad I made that decision because I've seen a lot of cons gas out and get attacked.

◊

When I first started playing, I didn't give a crap about winning, it was just a matter of survival. But the people who ran the league wanted things to be interesting. The losers would have to travel to the next city in a shitty run-down bus, shackled with the springs on the seats ready to pop out. We would also be placed in run down 'hotels' and served what resembled slop.

Now on the other hand the winners got a chance to ride in a first-class bus. The shackles were off, but the front did have a bulletproof barrier dividing the driver and guards from us. The bus even had a washroom, which was a luxury.

But I think the main luxury was back at the hotel. We had beautiful rooms—compared to what we were used to. The food was excellent, but the main thing was at night the guards would bring in booze, drugs and hookers. Now that is what I call incentive. I am not sure why they did this, but I guess the owners earned more money when their team won. Rumours were they made a huge profit off of betting and other rumours were winning teams got more of the gate revenue. Regardless of the reason, they wanted us to win, and they would dangle any carrot in front of us to achieve that goal.

When we won, I would allow myself one drink and no drugs. I didn't want anything affecting my health on the field. But I do love the ladies, and I would love as many as I could get my hands on. It was motivation for me to win, that's for sure.

I saw so many guys just go to town on the drugs and booze. I saw plenty of overdoses. The soldiers would just call for a doctor, but they wouldn't step in and tell us to keep the noise down or to slow down on the booze. The only time they would step in would be if one the inmates would start getting rough with one of the whores.

The dangerous thing about excessive partying was we never knew when our next game was. It could be the following day or the following week. Some dip shit that wakes up the next morning with a needle still in his arm, and numerous other drugs and alcohol in his system could either be hung over on a prison bus or hung over on the soccer pitch.

The guards didn't give a fuck if the player was curled up in the corner of the locker room, vomiting and shitting themselves. Teammates were forced to drag him out on the field. There was no sick days or injured reserve for players.

◊

One position we would rotate was goalie. Now I didn't care for being the goalie. I didn't like standing around then having to run at a moment's notice. I was always afraid of getting a leg cramp, or worse letting in a goal and having the players on my team heckling me for letting in a goal, "you fucking suck Shit Brains! If you let in another, I will kill you myself." Real camaraderie.

But some guys loved it because they could see the play in front of them, and always kept an eye on the zombies. Another reason is because a lot of them were lazy pricks. When it came down to saving the ball or saving yourself, self-preservation always won out.

One game we played was in Las Vegas. Now, Vegas sounds like a fun time; but you have to remember, we came in on a bus, and if we lost the last game it was a shitty bus. And plus, we were convicts. We didn't get time for sight-seeing.

We played a game in August and if you have ever been in Vegas in August you know it is hotter than hell. Coming from the northeast I don't get to experience this insane heat. One of the guys on our team told us to drink a lot.

There would be water bottles scattered along the side lines and behind the goals. He said it was easier to run with a water cramp than collapsing from heat stroke.

Anyways, I'm playing goal in this game and we had just lost three games in a row and had lost 8 players in that three-game span. The kick off started and like always, players are checking out the side lines waiting for the zombies. I stopped an easy shot when the roar of the crowd erupted. The goddamned zombies.

"Oh shit, niggers!" I muttered. They released two wiry looking black zombies.

Now it might sound racist saying, "Oh shit niggers" but this was coming from some black guys too. Some stereotypes carry over to zombies, and when you saw these tall, thin black zombies they looked fast. And let me tell you they were.

I kicked the ball down field and these two zombie fuckers came chasing after me. They never even looked at anyone else–it was if I had a bull's-eye on my chest. I bolted at the opposing players trying to lose them. Everyone ran away from me including the ref and I was left on my own.

These bastards were fast, and I did manage to lose one but for the entire first half, I shit you not, I had one chasing me. When it came to half time, we were allowed a 15-minute break. During breaks there was a caged-in shelter we would rest in. That is, if we could get to it. When the whistle is blown, the zombies don't give a shit. They don't stop and take it easy, they keep chasing.

When the whistle goes off that is when the 15-minute break begins, not when we all get in the shelter. Sometimes guys are so desperate to get in there they busted in even with a zombie on their ass. When a zombie gets in, it is trouble for everyone. I once saw six guys get bit in one shelter. Only four players finished the game on both sides. When shit like that starts to happen, you have to go on the offensive and start killing the zombies. Both sides team up and try to take out as many as we can.

That night in Vegas four of our guys barricaded the door because the zombies kept running around them. I didn't get a break in the shelter, but thankfully the zombies decided to chase someone else for five minutes.

I collapsed behind a goal where I spent about four minutes puking and heaving, and slowly sipping water before a zombie came after me again. The second half was much like the first. I was being chased from pillar to post–and didn't get a chance to save any shots other than the very first shot of the game.

We ended up losing the game, I can't remember the score–but I do remember that was the last game I was ever called, 'Shit Brains,' and I was never teased about going around full tilt at practice. I guess that is when the legend of 14 started. But really, I was just trying to save my ass, but the people who saw that game talk about it to this day.

◊

One of the big attractions was when women would be on the team. The prisons didn't really give a shit about women murders, just like they don't give a shit about the men. The crowd would always go ape shit when one of the women would get attacked, and they loved it even more when a female zombie would take out a man. I remember one bitch on our team, we nicknamed her 'Fuck Face'. Not very classy and not terribly original. You must remember this is a team made up of crude murderers.

Well this was Fuck Face's first game and she was all in tears in the locker room. After about half an hour of wailing and carrying on, a couple of the guys had already decided by the second half, if she wasn't dead by then, they would trip her or hit her from behind so they wouldn't have to put up with any more of her shit. There's no friends or sympathy among murderers.

Well, as soon as the zombies came out, they charged for Fuck Face because she started screaming and getting their attention. She started the run at the end of the stadium and the zombies were after her. When the zombies got closer the crowd got louder and more frantic expecting to see blood.

Fuck Face just dropped to her knees and covered her head. The crowd cheered and the zombies hearing all the noise ran over to the bulletproof glass and tried to get at the crowd. Zombies are stupid things. They can be distracted by noise, movement, something shiny, who the fuck knows? The crowd kept on pointing to Fuck Face and swearing at these zombies. She just cowered there until she realized she was not being attacked, and just got up and ran towards the other end of the stadium.

The only thing I remember from that game was during the second half one of our guys knocked her down and another kicked her in the head when she was down. The ref didn't see it because it happened behind his back. I'm not sure if he would have called a penalty since it was to one of our own players, but it was definitely unsportsmanlike conduct!

Anyways a zombie jumped on her and took a few bites, but she never got up. I think the kick to the head either killed her or put her in a coma. It may sound brutal, but this is a brutal 'game' with brutal people.

◊

One player I will always remember was Crazy. He got that name after he died. He only played a few games, but he made a lasting impression.

In the dressing room Crazy was a quiet guy, but most new players are quiet. They are either praying to their God, or just not wanting to piss themselves in front of their new teammates. You got to remember, prior to ending up playing, some of these guys were probably cheering in the stands.

One thing that is pretty common, which pisses off the fans, is going after the zombies, before they get you. The key is for someone to trip them up, and then someone to quickly kick them in the head or stomp on their neck. Now, there are risks. The first risk is for one of the fuckers to turn around just before you trip them. Another is when they are down, someone kicks, and blood goes flying. If you ingest it or get it into your eyes, you become one of *them*.

One thing the fans will never see is the shower room. After a game there are two heavily armed soldiers standing at the shower entrance with guns pointing at us. I guess they think one of us may have a delayed reaction turning into a zombie; I don't know. But what I do know is *every one of us* moves very slowly and usually soaps with one hand while the other is in the air. Zombies don't act calm, and we want to act as calm as a summer breeze. The last thing we ever wanted was some dick to suddenly turn and go "boo" to the guards. A quick trigger finger would finish us all.

So, getting back to Crazy. He earned his nickname in his very first game. When we saw what he did someone muttered, "Man that guy is crazy!" It was true and the name stuck.

It was the beginning of the game and the ball is being kicked around with eyes scanning the sideline entrance and waiting for the crowd to erupt. All of a sudden, the zombies come out and Crazy b-lines it right to them. One darted to the left but the other zombie was going right for Crazy.

Just before they bash head on, Crazy jumps in the air and drop kicks the zombie. With the zombie stunned, Crazy gets up and starts stomping down on the zombie's face and neck with his cleats. Blood is starting to flow and spray but Crazy just kept on stomping laughing the entire time.

Most of us just stood there in awe watching, while trying to keep an eye on the other zombie. Crazy then went chasing after the other zombie. He caught up and tripped the fuck and again proceeded to stomp and jump up and down on its head. None of us got near, because of all the blood. We were sure Crazy was going to get infected.

But to our pleasure both zombies were dead and Crazy never turned. We just played soccer for the next 90 minutes and laughed and had a great time. The fans on the other hand, hated it. They booed and screamed at us. They started chanting for another zombie, but they only bring two to a game. I guess they are safer with smaller numbers.

By the time we were finished the stadium was nearly empty with only a few hecklers remaining. We wanted to pat Crazy on the back, but he was covered in blood, and none of us wanted to risk touching him.

The scariest part about that game was the shower. The guards had their guns set on Crazy just because of the shear amount of blood that was on him, and we thought for sure he may do something stupid like try to scare the guards. But to Crazy's credit he just soaped himself off and waited under the showerhead until we got the all clear to dry off and change.

When we got to our hotel the booze, blow and bitches were waiting for us. Crazy never bothered with the women in the short time he was around. But goddamn, did he love the cocaine. We thought for sure he was going to OD due to the number of lines he snorted back joyfully. But come morning time he was sitting in a leather chair, facing the window, watching the sun come up. The man's constitution must have been as crazy as he was.

In his next game, we were playing down in Texas. Most of our team was not from New York, just a couple of us. When one of our guys would die, they would just fill the roster from someone from death row in the state we were in. The fans never cared about local boys representing their state. They just wanted to see us die. Period.

This time during the game Crazy never went after the zombies. We were both relieved and disappointed. A lot of us figured he couldn't do it two games in a row, but the idea of having another easy game was appealing to us. What Crazy did this time shocked us even more. Crazy was zig zagging along the field just running with his arms stretched out to the side, like a child pretending to be an airplane.

While he was playing airplane, the rest of us were looking for the zombies. Anyways Crazy ran alongside the ref and in one swift move threw a haymaker that dropped the son of a bitch.

One thing we don't do is go after refs. Now there are no rules or penalties for attacking or killing a ref, but there are risks. First of all, if we get too close, some of the fuckers like using the taser to take us down and watch the zombies attack us. I've seen some refs run up behind players and taser them right at the base of the skull. The player drops like a ton of bricks and starts to convulse. Sometimes the player can get up, sometimes not.

Referees also love payback. If a ref knows a player tried to fuck with a fellow ref, he will be out to get you, and will give you two quick cards, so the poor bastard has to run around with 50-pounds on him. If you survive that game, the ref in the next game might give you two quick cards and there you go again with 50-pounds on you. Sooner or later you're fucked. Fucking with a ref equals a death sentence.

Crazy didn't give a shit. He gave the ref a kick in the head then just trotted off as if nothing had happened. The roar of the crowd was a mix of anger and pleasure. Some of them show up to see whatever violence they could get. Every so often I think we would had been better off as a society if we had been completely over run with zombies or had an asteroid make us as extinct as the dinosaurs. We live in a sick fucking world.

Needless to say, the zombies got the ref. They bit at him a few times and then ran off. The ref turned into a zombie, but he was all fucked up. He kept on falling down and stumbling all over the pitch. The kick to the head turned out to be lethal because by the second half the ref laid dead in front of one of the goals. Fortunately for us he died in front of the other teams net, and none of their players wanted to risk being too close to it. We won the game and once again Crazy went crazy on the cocaine that night.

He only played three games for us Crazy did. In his final game he truly and forever earned his nickname. It was like a replay of his first game. This time the fans were truly excited because one of the zombies was a woman.

Crazy went heading straight for the zombies and this time both saw him and went straight for him. Again, Crazy did a drop kick to the male zombie, quickly got up and nailed the female with a punch to her face that knocked the bitch out. He strolled over to the male zombie and again with enthusiasm stomped the shit out of the thing, killing it.

Next, he walked over to the zombie bitch. But he didn't start stomping he just stood down looking at her and just started rubbing his crotch. "Holy shit he's going to fuck her," I said. But Crazy just kept on playing with himself looking down at her. I think even some blood seekers in the crowd were starting to feel uncomfortable.

But then the scariest look I had ever seen happened when Crazy turned around and scanned all of us with an evil look in his eye. He suddenly jumped on the zombie and started to rip apart her throat with his teeth. The crowd went ape shit, and we just stared not believing our eyes. When he got up, he had a creepy as fuck smile on his face, but now he was a zombie.

In one of the most devastating games I have ever witnessed he killed the ref, the entire Texan team, and all but five of our players. He never let any of the players he attacked become zombies, he made sure he killed each and every one. I could tell by the look in his eyes he wanted to kill us all by himself.

To this day I have no idea what ever happened with Crazy after the game. I don't know if soldiers killed him or used him in other games. We never found out. We just get packed up and are sent to the next game, with no news of the past and no hope for the future.

◊

To say time passes slowly is an understatement. So, I was shocked to find out one day, I was playing in my 10th year. Honestly, I felt I had been playing all my life. I considered myself one of the best players on our team because a lot of my teammates who had more skill would eventually die, and I actually got pretty good at the game. I tried my hardest every game to score because I wanted to end up in bed with some whore and ride in a comfortable bus.

I heard somewhere the longest a player ever survived the league before me was six-years. There was no fanfare or golden watch for me. Stepping out onto the pitch is a death sentence, and for 10-years the Grim Reaper was waiting patiently for me to trip up.

The fact I had made it that long is incredible. Considering we usually played every two or three nights and there was no off-season. There was no championship game, and I don't even think they had standings or had stats on players. The fact I managed not to pull any muscles, get tripped up by my own feet while being chased by a zombie or have some other player trip me up was a miracle. Also, if you got sick, you never sat out a game. You were pushed out onto the field with a small head cold or pneumonia—the authorities never cared, and neither did the fans.

But around that time, I noticed a few fans yelling out "14" to me. Usually we got swore at with a lot of, "Hope you die tonight." So, the fact that a few people yelled out my jersey number was a weird change.

Also new players coming onto our team called me 14. I started my 'career' known as Shit Brains and now I was just a number. I found out from some of the players, when they were on the outside, they had seen a piece about me on the state-run TV. I guess there was a lot of interest in a murderer who seemed to cheat death for so long. They didn't make me into a hero, but it drew a lot of attention from the fans.

It seemed each game, more and more people started yelling my number. A lot of the fans still wanted to see me die, because the bastards would cheer every time a zombie went after me and from the field, I could hear a collective let down when the zombie broke off his chase to go after someone else. It was strange after hearing the moans of disappointment in my survival I heard some cheers for my success.

Soon when we would enter the stadium, I would notice soldiers nudging each other and pointing in my direction. I could see them silently mouth "14." I could really care less about the notoriety. As far as my 'fans' they could go fuck themselves because only a short time earlier they were hoping to see my blood spilled all over the place. I could give two shits what the soldiers thought. They were a bunch of power-hungry fucks that sold their souls a long time ago.

But the one thing I did love about the whole rising popularity of 14 was the whores! They fucking loved me! I was the next big thing to a star and they always wanted a piece of me. My teammates hated it, but they understood. There was a lot of respect for me, with what I have gone through over the years. For that I am forever grateful. It would have taken only one spiteful prick to trip me up, but they never did. The only people I could trust were convicted murderers! What a fucked-up world.

You would think over the years I met a lot of interesting people. Well, yes, I did, but I never got a chance to know any of the men or women I played with. I remember one guy I played with—I have no idea what his name was, and he never lasted long enough to earn a nickname. Hell, at this point so many faces have died in front of me, they all kind of blur into one.

Anyways, this guy, as soon as he entered the locker room he started to shake. I knew he would die that game. It was not the kind of shake with survival mode adrenaline pumping through the body, but a shake of meeting one's fate. You learn that shake after so many years.

Well this dude is sitting on the bench putting on his cleats repeating, "I didn't do it. I didn't kill my wife." I'm not a priest and neither are any of the other players on the team, and it really pisses us off when someone wants to confess to us, as if we give a shit. What do these assholes expect from us? Do they think we are going to get one of the soldiers and tell them a horrible mistake was made? Do they think we will protect them? Out there, as much as we try to help one another, it is every man for himself. If you try to be a hero and save someone else, you may end up dead.

So, this guy gets onto the field and when the game starts he is quietly weeping saying he didn't do it. Well, the roar of the crowd lets us know the fucking zombies are out. This guy grabs my jersey and yells, "I didn't kill my wife! I didn't do it!"

I could tell in his eyes he is telling the truth. But the bitch of it is: that all through history plenty of innocent people have been sentenced to death for something they never did, and this guy wasn't going to be the last. I pulled away from him, still keeping eye contact and told him, "I believe you." Then I ran like a son of a bitch.

I think he may have lasted about 15-minutes or so. The zombies only had a quick chew on him before they ran after someone else. While he was still down, I ran up and stomped on his neck, breaking it. One rule of this game is killing them before they get a chance to get up. If too many zombies are running around, we would all be dead.

I also remember this one guy who joined the team and said he used to run marathons all the time. He bragged about how he could outrun any goddamn zombie. I had met a lot of healthy killers during my time, and a lot claim they can run all day. But the truth is luck plays a big part in it. Sometimes, if you zig instead of zag and you become a zombie snack.

Well in Mr. Marathon's first game, we had a fat zombie and a dumpy looking bitch zombie come out. Now I want to say, I don't think the army keeps a shit load of zombies in a giant pen in a military complex for these games. I think it is safer to say, they get junkies, thieves or sex offenders and give them the virus before the game. Hell, I am sure a lot of them were people who spoke out against the army, trying to restore democracy.

So, the fat zombie and the frumpy bitch were jogging around trying to chase us. The crowd was pissed. They liked it more when there were sleek looking nigger zombies chasing us, because they figured they would be fast, and we would end up dead. That or hot looking female zombies.

After the first half the zombies couldn't catch a cold and I focused on scoring because I wanted to bang a whore that night. Well doesn't Mr. I Eat All My Fruits And Vegetables come trotting by me looking at me saying this was easy as pie. The dipshit wasn't looking and ran right into the frumpy, ugly bitch knocking them both down. The bitch sat up stunned and immediately jumped on Mr. Fucking Healthy himself chomping down on him. She stayed on top of him until the fat fuck waddled over and started eating as well.

Now it's rare that a zombie will totally feed on a player. Rarer still that both zombies will chow down. The rest of the half they chewed and slobbered on Mr. This Is Easy As Pie. With about 10 minutes left in the game the soccer ball got kicked and stopped right in the middle of the two suckling zombies.

Neither team wanted to get near them and when the ref told us to get it, we just simply told him to fuck off. What was he going to do? Give us a yellow card and wear a 25-pound jacket just to stand off on the side and watch them gorge. For the last ten minutes the crowd booed, and we stood around like hyenas watching lions eat a zebra.

I also had a chance to play with this smoking hot stripper once. I think she was in there for killing her boyfriend or something. Let me tell you, this chick was hot! The crowd used to go ape shit for her, watching that tight little ass run around the pitch with her tits bouncing up and down. It was a thing of beauty.

I tried everything to get into this broad's pants. But she didn't go for it. When we won her vice was vodka, and that bitch loved vodka. It was eventually her demise of course. We won and unfortunately for her we had a game the next day and ol' Tits McGee drank her sorrows away the night before.

When game time came around, she looked pale and had the dry heaves. Hard to run when you are doing that. It didn't really take long for her to change into a zombie. Even as a zombie she was suffering with the hangover and was not much of a threat. In all I think she lasted about 10 games or so. Too bad really. I really wanted to bang her, and I thought her will to live would break after a few more games. Why not fuck, if you are going to die soon anyways?

◊

I played in extreme heat, torrential rain, blizzard like conditions and wicked winds. I should have died a thousand times over but for whatever reason I survived. Some say God is looking out for me; part of me thinks he is punishing me. You never lose that sick feeling before stepping on the field and when you hear the roar of the crowd cheering for the zombies. I heard that roar in my dreams every night.

Young convicts, new to the team, would always come up to me and say, "14? Can you give me some advice for out there?" I used to try to mentor some of them, but I stopped. Why bother when they always ended up dead. Sometimes they would last one-game, sometimes one-year; but they always ended up dead. And me? I just kept playing. The '14' mania seemed to get bigger each passing year.

The fans would scream for me just like they did for the zombies. I guess by that point I was a zombie. My life consisted of running away from death, day after day after day. There were no other thoughts. I didn't dream about my life after soccer. I no longer thought about my life before I started playing, but I did in my dreams.

I always dreamed of this little girl watching me on the sidelines. The zombies and players would always run past her, if she were invisible. But I always saw her. She had the saddest eyes I ever seen. When I would make direct eye contact with her a shiver would slice up my spine.

"You killed me daddy. Why did you kill me?"

I would slow down to a trot. Around me players were panicking, running in every direction, some were screaming.

"I would have been a good girl. I would have loved you. Why didn't you love me daddy?"

She lowered her head and slowly wept. I turned my head and saw a zombie running towards me. Spit rolling down his chin and that crazy look in his eyes. But I never ran, I would look back at the little girl.

She would look back up at me, and suddenly her eyes were the warmest blue eyes I had ever seen, full of life and love. I wanted to be lost in her eyes forever.

"Goodbye daddy."

Then the zombie would tackle me, and I would wake, shaking and tears in my eyes. I don't pay too much attention to dreams, but if I were to ask what sex the unborn child was when I killed it, I would bet my life they would come back and say it would have been a girl.

◊

One day I woke up and realized I had been playing this 'game' for 20-years. Twenty fucking years of being chased by zombies, seeing death all around me and hearing the blood lust from the crowd!

Each day it was harder for me to get up. My muscles were sore and my will to live was almost gone. Before each game I would say to myself that maybe I should just kneel on the grass, close my eyes and wait for the zombies. I think the only reason I never did was the fear of them not killing me.

If they turned me into a zombie, I would be a bigger sideshow. People would come out just to watch '14 the zombie'. Plus, what if part of me was still alive in that zombie, and I was still running, playing the game, trapped inside this possessed body?

So, I just kept going. Like a robot going from city to city never to see anything but the inside of a bus, a hotel and a stadium. I know

I'm going to sound like a perv, but one of the only things that kept me going was the whores. If we lost a bunch of games the depression would be heavy. Risking our lives for nothing. At least with the whores it was some human contact. I was never going to be free, but when I was with one of the women–I was free.

It was in Ohio when I saw the soldier in the suit come into the locker room. I knew it was a soldier by the way the prick was walking. I could spot one of those fuckers from a mile away. This asshole may not be with the military any more, or maybe just sits behind a desk, but he was still military to me. And I hated him.

My teammates watched him walk into the room. No one ever entered the locker room unless it was a soldier in uniform, always with a gun. This fuck just strolled over to me. "Mr. Cooke?" was all he asked.

I had not heard my name for so long I had forgotten it. For a moment I thought he had the wrong person. "Yeah?" I wanted to ignore him or tell him to fuck off and leave me alone, but truth be told, I was just as curious as the rest of the guys as to why he was here.

"Mr. Cooke, you have ten-games left to play. After the ten-games you will be a free man. Your first of ten games will be tonight."

I just stared at him. I heard what he said, but my brain could not register it. I wanted to know if this was some sick game the military was playing on me. I wanted to know if this was part of my punishment besides having to be chased by zombies and seeing people die around me all the time. "Is this some sick fucking joke? Huh?" was all I could come out with.

"Consider this your parole Mr. Cooke. After 10-games you will be a free man." Then the prick left. When I saw him come in I hated him. When I saw him leave, part of me still hated him, but part of me wanted to hug him.

I just sat there stunned. My teammates were stunned too. After leaving me with my thoughts for a couple of minutes they came over and gave me a pat on the shoulder and offered their congratulations. I just wished he had told me on my very last game that I was done instead of a stupid fucking countdown. I was scared every single time I stepped out onto the soccer pitch, thinking today might be my last day on earth. But now I was thinking about the future instead of the present. It was if the Grim Reaper was snickering in the corner at the idea of me dying only days away from freedom. After so many years of chasing me, he could now touch me with his bony finger.

I was surprised I didn't get killed that 10th game from freedom. I just couldn't help but think about what the military prick had said to me. There was no way I was going to be a free man, was I? The crowd went wild when I went onto the field. I was a legend of the game, and I hated them for it.

There were signs in the crowd for me, but no 'congratulations' signs. Just the usually '14' and a few '14 you die tonight!' The crowd would usually yell insults and prophesied my demise. But that night I thought they might have known something. Did they know something I didn't? Was the fix in for me, or did these people have a psychic premonition?

I almost got done-in right away. I was too busy looking around and thinking about things I almost got plowed into by a zombie. I ran as fast as I could. At this point in my life I had terrific stamina. I could run all game no problems. The problem was, is I had lost a lot of speed over the years, and a foot race with a fully rested zombie was not a good idea for an older fart like myself.

I just started booting it, and like so many cons before me I zigged instead of zagged. I made a quick turn and I was headed right at the ref. The sick fuck had his taser pointed right at the middle of my chest. I slid hoping for the best. Lucky for me the ref ended up tasering the zombie behind me, knocking it down and temporarily out.

The ref was proud of himself and he looked down at me giving me a dirty look. I could tell the son of a bitch wished he could have gotten me too. I got up and started to stomp on the zombie breaking its neck.

Later in the game I scored the game-winning goal when a crossing pass bounced off my face, breaking my nose, and the ball found the back of the net. I was too busy looking around for the remaining zombie to keep an eye on the ball.

After the goal none of my teammates came close to me. My nose was bleeding all down my jersey, and one-thing players are going to avoid anyone who is bleeding. Blood equals contamination, which equals zombie. An easy equation.

After the game we rushed back to the locker room and the military pricks had their guns trained on me. I thought they were going to kill me, when I remembered my broken nose. Blood scares the shit out of the guards as well. I stood in the shower with my arms up and let the water wash the blood from my face. I didn't even bother using soap, because I didn't want to freak out the guards with any sudden movements.

I had to stay in the showers long after the others left. My fucking nose kept on bleeding. Thankfully and finally a doctor came in and gave me some gauze to pack my nose.

When we got back to the hotel room, a nice one since we had won, I headed straight to the liquor and took a quick shot. I needed something to calm my nerves. I was a wreck. I thought about pouring another, but I didn't. In all these years I never took any more than one drink, so that part was superstition. The other reason was, if I took another drink, I might not have stopped.

I even looked over at the cocaine, heroin, magic mushrooms, acid tablets, pot and assorted pills that were on the table. That could ease my mind and set me on a trip. My luck I would OD, or go on some fucked up, paranoid trip, and I was paranoid as it was.

I didn't even bother with any of the whores. My mind was racing, thinking things over, wondering what I was going to do. I don't know if I could have even got it up. I just wondered to an empty corner and sat in a faux leather recliner and just thought about how I was going to stay alive another nine games.

◊

Somehow, I managed to survive nine of the games, and I sat in the locker room for what I hoped to be my last one. The prick in the suit never came back, and none of the soldiers ever said anything to me. There was no acknowledgement from the crowd, so they were probably not told.

My teammates knew and I could see them peaking over at me from time to time. No one sat close to me–I guess I know how a baseball pitcher is feeling in the last innings of a game sitting in the dugout with a no-hitter on the line. None of the other players wanted to jinx him.

I stepped out onto the pitch and I heard the crowd erupt chanting '14'. I took some deep breaths after the whistle blew and waited for the zombies. It didn't take long until I heard the roar of the crowd to know they had come onto the field.

To my amazement I saw my teammates run to the side line, flanking the zombies. Some of them were decoys for distraction while the others came up from behind. When they did, they tripped the zombie up and quickly started stomping down on its neck and body until it stopped moving. The exact same thing happened to the other zombie.

When they were finished, they pointed at me. I knew what they had done. Besides royally pissing off the fans, they did it for me. For my final game, I was guaranteed to survive. My teammates came to me, hugged me and said, 'that was for you.'

We ended up losing that game, but I didn't think my teammates minded. They smiled knowing they saved one of their own and gave a big fuck you to the powers that be. There was no mention of it being my final game. No mention of it on the score board, no confetti after the final whistle. Fuck them.

Before I got into the locker room, I was whisked away by gun toting soldiers. I didn't even have a chance to say goodbye to the guys. The led me down a hallway that was deserted and into an empty room. I thought I was dead. They were going to kill me because my team showed them up. That or the whole going free thing was bullshit. My teammates would never know I was dead; they would just assume I was released.

In the corner of the room was the military prick with the suit. He nodded towards an adjoining room, "go in there and shower. We have clothes for you in the corner. Hurry up because we are on a schedule."

It was the fastest shower I think I had ever taken. I changed into a pair of jeans and a simple shirt. They led me down a hall into a van and I was driven away from the stadium for the first time in 20-years in something that wasn't a prison bus.

The prick informed me they were taking me to my apartment. They provided me with a job, which I would report to in three days, and I had a bank account with a small amount of money. They handed me my identification and a key to my apartment. The van stopped in front of a building and the door was opened for me.

"It is apartment 1414 Mr. Cooke," the prick said with a smug look on his face. "You are also invited to attend a game next week. VIP seats. Be there."

And the van took off. I stood on the sidewalk watching it until it was out of sight. That was it. Again, I expected some kind of fanfare, maybe some fans waiting for me at the front door—a couple of hookers would have been nice too. Fuck them.

I looked up and down the street and finally walked into the apartment.

◊

Entering the stadium was the weirdest feeling. For years we entered through the shipping and receiving doors. Now I walked in through the main gates. I recognized the buzz in the crowd as I made my way towards my gate.

I asked a soldier where my seat was, and he led me to it. I believe he had no idea who I was, and he led me to a boxed suite. When I entered, I saw what looked to be military brass, with all their shinny medals on their chest. A few smirked at me when I walked in, but nobody talked to me. All the better. I hated the looks of these pricks and knew I wouldn't be striking up any pleasant conversations.

I took my seat and looked around the stadium. This was my first time getting out of my apartment, other than going to the shitty job I had. The world had changed and so had I. I couldn't make friends with anyone, because I imagined them in the stands while I was playing, cheering for my death and of my fellow cons.

I almost didn't hear the players coming on to the field. There was a big chorus of boos and no chanting for '14'. As for as 14 he was gone. There was no mention of me in the press—I was just gone. As far as people were concerned, I was dead. Probably shanked by one of my fellow inmates or died in my sleep. I was not recognized by anyone on the outside, just the military pricks in this box suite that ignored me and occasionally looked over at me and chuckled to themselves.

It was the roar of the crowd that woke me out of my daydream. The zombies had run onto the field. The players just scrambled for their lives and the fans loved it. I just watched in shock. After years of playing I had no idea of what it looked like, how scared we were.

My vision started to blur until I realized I was crying. I wiped my eyes and looked around and I saw the military pricks smiling at me with their shit eating grins. I ran out of the box followed by their laughter. I wish I would have gone back in there and killed them all, but I had to get away. I couldn't stand to see or hear the game.

I ran down the ramp towards the exits as fast as I could go. I saw a man running up with who appeared to be his son. They took their fucking kids to see this? The idea of letting children watch this horror made me hate the fans more. I wished them all to die. Where was God to smite this den of sin?

As I ran down the spiralling ramp, I noticed a soldier who was watching me get onto the radio. Soldiers are a very jumpy breed and a man running like a crazy person, crying, may bring fear upon men with guns. They might believe something was wrong and would begin firing. The guards I was running to have full authority to shut down the stadium. That would mean every exit would be airtight. If you got caught in the way of these doors you were dead. They were meant to shut regardless if someone was pinned between them, you would get ripped in two.

I was getting near the bottom of the ramp, just a couple of more turns and there would be some jittery soldiers, tipped off by another jittery soldier. I tried to force myself to stop but I couldn't. A huge roar from the crowd made me cry out. I recognized that cheer–a zombie had caught someone. The con was soon to be dead or a zombie.

Finally, just before the corner I managed to stop running; but I could not stop the tears. The soldiers just chuckled when they saw the tears in my eyes and let me though the exit without any questions. Over the years they had seen plenty of people who couldn't take the blood and gore, and to them, I was one of them. Just another pussy.

I just kept walking until I came to a grassy area and fell to my knees and crawled to a small tree. I wrapped my arms around the tree as if I was a small boy with my arms wrapped around my mommy's or daddy's leg. As I held the tree I cried hysterically, but not for the men who were running for their lives in the stadium behind me. It was not for the men and women that played beside me and died instead of me. It was not for the life of the woman, man and unborn child I took. I cried for myself.

For all the years I wanted to cry before, during and after a game. When I wanted to cry riding to and from games in a shitty bus, or in the arms of some strange whore. I let it all out now.

Selfishly I cried just for me, outside of a stadium of death, alone in an unfamiliar world.

Powder or Oil

The buzzer for the dryer rang signalling that the towels were dry, waiting for a new load. She took the dry ones out and put wet ones in; but she wouldn't worry about this load. She'd empty it in the morning. She just wanted to fold these, stock up the shelves and close up. It was another tedious day.

Lin knew working here was merely a speed bump on the road of life. Unfortunately some speed bumps are bigger than others and come out of nowhere.

From an early age she wanted to go to America. She wanted to live the American dream and be a part of Hollywood. An American family lived down the street near her house in Beijing. She made friends with the children and would spend hours watching old American movie classics. Grace Kelly was her hero. Lin had watched all her movies and was obsessed with High Society.

Lin loved Hollywood and wanted to be a part of the scene, but she was realistic too. The women who starred in the movies she loved never looked like her. If she were to make it in front of the screen, she would either be a stand-in or she would be cast for her Asian appearance and not because of any acting skills.

That truth was okay with Lin. She would be happy working behind the camera's supporting in any way she could. She didn't care if it was makeup, lighting or catering. She just wanted to be a part of the movie machine.

She worked devotedly at her English. If... *when* she arrived in America, she wanted to hit the pavement running, and being fluent in English would be a huge advantage. Unfortunately, getting to America was easier said than done.

There was a long line of people waiting to immigrate to America ahead of her. Many with sponsors in America and their sponsors had a lot of money. She had neither a sponsor nor money, so her chances seemed slim. She was a determined, but impatient young woman.

She was rejected for a U.S. visa and was frustrated at the roadblocks she was facing. Every day that passed was another day away from her Hollywood dream. She knew those days could easily become years and before she knew it, her dream would be over.

Lin was working at a local market when she expressed her frustrations to a co-worker. The co-worker remained quiet but a couple of days later approached Lin with another option.

The woman's uncle knew a guy, who knew a guy that could help her out. She passed Lin a phone number and said she was to ask for Heng. When the number was passed over the woman walked away and would not speak any more on the subject.

Lin considered waiting a couple of days to think about what seemed to be a cloak and dagger arrangement, but curiosity got the best of her. When she called and asked for Heng, she was given a location to meet and was told to wear a yellow hat. The man on the other line hung up after the simple instructions.

Black-market transit to America was always in the back of her mind. Run by criminals in both China and America they would sneak Chinese nationals in. Lin had considered this option but was wary of dealing with the criminal underground and the amount of money it would take to get these types of people to help her. But now that the opportunity fell into her lap, she had to try.

On the day of the meet she wore the yellow hat and waited patiently for Heng to show up. When she had given up hope a woman approached her. The woman looked Lin over and asked her to stand up and turn fully around. When she was told to sit back down the woman slipped a piece of paper into Lin's hand.

"Come to this address on Friday," the woman said without introducing herself. "Say goodbye to whoever you need to. You will be coming to get your picture taken—look nice, but not too nice." Lin wanted to ask what that meant, but the woman continued. "Once we have forged your new ID, you will be on a ship to America. That is if you have money?"

"How much?" Lin asked feeling both desperate and excited.

"All that you have." The woman walked away ignoring Lin's follow up questions.

If she was going to jump into the fire she decided she was going to jump in with both feet. Lin said her farewells to her family. She didn't tell any friends because the less people knew the better. She sold everything she had and hoped it would be enough. With butterflies in her stomach and a prayer of hope on her lips she went to the address and had her fake ID produced. The people she was dealing with were impressed with her perfect English so they made her an American birth certificate, passport, drivers license and social security card.

"I'm going to be an American!" she screamed inside her head. The man who took her photo talked to her as he quickly packed up his equipment, "When you get to America go to a bookstore and learn American history. If people are going to believe you're American, you'll have to be knowledgeable. Also, learn about the city of birth on your new ID and the State history too. Sometimes it can be the most basic thing that can arouse suspicions."

He led her to the back door where there were a couple of men waiting. The photographer handed over an envelope that contained her ID to the men, and they led her to a waiting car. They drove her to the port and Lin was introduced to her means of travel. She didn't know what to expect, but the giant cargo ship was not what she had in mind. On the dock she entered a cargo container which she shared with 12 other people. The container was far from being a luxury suite, but there were enough supplies to survive.

There was an air purification unit that ran on batteries. Small holes that were concealed with a removable metal plate insured they wouldn't die from lack of oxygen. Sleeping bags were rolled in one of the corners and at the far end was a small divider with a stack of simple five gallon pails for a toilet.

There was battery powered lights that ran during the day and fortunately for Lin she brought a couple of paperbacks with her, to help pass time and keep her mind off the claustrophobia that was always lurking in the back of her mind. During the night, the lights were turned off and the metal plates were removed to let the container air out.

The 22-day voyage seemed like a lifetime; but she finally arrived in America!

She was driven to a dull grey building in the heart of San Francisco's China Town. She was taken to the second floor and told, "This is where you will work and the room above is where you will live until you pay off your debt."

"What debt!"

Lin was told she owed $20,000 dollars for the ID's. The money she gave in China barely covered her "transportation". She was to work giving massages until she raised enough money to buy back her identification. She was told in plain language, if she tried to run or seek help she would be hurt and her loved ones in China would be killed. The harder she worked the quicker she could pay off her debt.

"Oh, by the way," added her now captives, "you will be charged $100 a day in rent."

It didn't take her long to find out that this 'massage parlour', was more of a rub and tug. The odd time she would just give a massage but most of the men would want their pathetic penises rubbed, and then spill their disgusting seed all over her hand.

She didn't hate men, but she found them very sad and shameless. She couldn't possibly see herself in a relationship with a man anytime soon. Lin had no desire to become a lesbian, but if she had to spend any more time satisfying these perverts, she just might give it a shot.

She had finished stocking the rooms and came out to the reception area when she was startled by a man. He was standing by the desk, standing very ridged. Something appeared very off about him.

"Sorry we're closed," said Lin to the tall white man. Most of her clients were Asian but she had her share of customers who were black and white. Regardless of the colour, most men were pigs.

The man's teeth were gritted together when he spoke, "Please! I need you to bend and crack my arms. Please, I'm so stiff. There's a $100 in my front shirt pocket if you do."

Lin didn't trust the man. Her time in America spent jerking off men, didn't exactly build up trust in them. The man's eyes were gentle enough, but that didn't mean a thing. Yang Xinhai killed and raped over 70 victims back home in China, and he seemed to have gentle eyes. She slowly reached to the man's pocket and he didn't move or say anything. Like he promised, in his pocket was a new $100 bill. It was easy money, and she *needed* money. She agreed and tucked the money into her bra.

She took hold of his arm and he was extremely tense. She tried to bend his arm at the elbow but faced some resistance. A little moan escaped the man and she applied more pressure. A loud POP erupted from his elbow. The man gave a gasp, not a gasp of pain or pleasure, but more of relief.

Lin took a step backwards and the man pleaded. "No, no, no! Please continue! Please, I'm okay," he said with gritted teeth. Reluctantly she grabbed his arm again afraid she broke something or was going to break him.

Smaller pops and grinding sounds came from his elbow until it moved freely. It reminded Lin of one of her favorite movies not starring Grace Kelly. The Wizard of Oz. She felt as if she was Dorothy and this stranger was the Tin Man. Instead of a can of oil, she just helped crack the man's stiff joints.

She moved down the wrist and was sickened by the noise. How could anyone be so stiff? But he pleaded with gritted teeth and she twisted, and pulled back and forth on his wrist. The fingers were bent and pulled back with sickening POPS coming from every knuckle. The feeling of the cracking in her hands, sent cold chills down her spine.

The worst part was the shoulder. With a lot of pressure she lifted his arm in the air. CRACK! She jumped back absolutely certain she had dislocated the man's shoulder. "No, no! It's perfect. Please continue," he said with jaws clinched.

Lin lifted his arms in different angles and the popping and grinding continued, but not as severe as the original tortured sound of the shoulder. She was able to move his arm in big windmill movements and the man moaned in obvious relief.

"Can you please do the other arm?"

"No. No, I have to close up now."

"Please!" he pleaded the words slightly muffled between his clinched jaw. "There's another $100 in my shirt pocket!"

She couldn't resist the temptation of the money. Lin took the $100 from his shirt pocket, put the money into her bra and worked on his other arm. CRACK, POP, GRIND. The same sounds and the same extreme stiffness. What was wrong with this man? He was still standing stiff as a board—how did he manage to make his way to the second floor? There was no elevator.

When both arms were cracked and manipulated with a free range of motion restored with no grinding or resistance, the man asked her to crack his back. He said he would lie on the floor and all she had to do was walk up and down his back. Again, she protested no; but the man said he had $500 in his back pocket if she would do it. The power of money swayed her to do it, but she never wondered how he had all this money, and why he just didn't get the money out of his back pocket since his arms were moving freely.

The man fell flat on his face on the floor in front of her. She let out a scream. The stranger never even put his hands out to break his fall. "It's okay, I'm fine. Please, just help with my back. Take the money," he said with a muffled voice.

Lin held her hands over her mouth in complete shock. She was sure the man would have broken his nose, or even knocked out some teeth. But he lay on the floor, nose to the ground, still talking through gritted teeth, offering her a huge amount of money she considered leaving the man here and running out the doors, but it *was* a large amount of money.

Money she could use to buy her freedom and move to Hollywood. She would take acting lessons there–just in case, because you never know. As well she could find out what careers were in demand in the movie industry and work towards learning a trade if needed. Her dream was closer with each dollar she earned.

She took the money and placed it in the cup of her bra. She stepped up onto the man and the cracking started right away. She could feel the spine crunching under her feet. But the man's moans of relief and pleas of encouragement kept her working up and down his back. It only took a couple of minutes to earn her $500 and she could tell the man was feeling better. Though he was still talking with his jaw clinched, she could hear some tension come out of his voice (even with his face still pressed against the floor), his breathing seemed deeper and calmer.

The stranger again asked for her services. He wanted his legs worked on. Lin thought the man must have a serious medical condition and should see a doctor about this, not her. But once again her thoughts were distracted when he said he had $500 in his other back pocket. She took the money, slipped it into her bra and helped turn him over onto his back. She expected to see a bloody nose, but he was none the worse for wear.

The process didn't take long but she felt nauseous with feeling and hearing the joints popping. She started to lift the straightened leg up and heard a tremendous POP. She moved from one leg to the next repeating the movements. CRACK, POP of the knees before they finally moved freely. She took off his shoes and started to rotate his foot. The grinding was sickening, but faded with each movement. She cracked his toes and pushed up and down on his foot trying to get a full range of motion.

The worst had to be the hips. She had his knees bent and leaned in with her weight while pushing the knees down towards the ground. POP! His hips sounded like a shotgun going off. She flinched and moved away certain she had broken his leg or dislocated his hips. The man gasped at the sound but sighed in relief after it was done.

She stood up and looked down at the man who had started to rise. Surprisingly, there were still a number of cracks and pops. The man stood up straight and though she couldn't see it from his mouth she could see the smile in his eyes.

"We're almost done, and thank you very much! It feels so much better. I just need my neck cracked along with my jaw."

Lin put her hands up in front of her waving no. "You can do that. I don't want to hurt you and make a mistake and you end up paralyzed or something." The last thing she needed to do was hurt this strange man and him ended up in the hospital with an injury because of her. If the police got involved they would investigate her and possibly find out her identification was fake.

The police could also investigate the massage parlour and the other girls. There was always a threat the business could be shut down and everyone sent back to China. If she ended up being the cause of that, her life and the life of her family was in jeopardy.

"Ridiculous," the man said through his teeth. "You are fantastic! Do this for $1000, it's in my front pocket. Do *this* and we're done—I'm an extremely generous tipper." Greed won out and defeated any fears she had.

She could see the money in his shirt pocket and Lin took it out and counted it. She looked at him again and nodded in agreement as she stored the money in her bra that was now well padded with bills.

If she wasn't so focused on the money, she could have heard that little voice in the back of her mind. The voice asking why he had so much money and where was all this money coming from. This is the third time she has taken money out of his shirt pocket. There was no way she didn't miss $1000 the last time she took money out of it. How did it get in there?

Lin slowly moved his head side to side. CRACK, CRACK. She pulled her hands back, but the man said he was fine, and she was doing excellent. After a couple of minutes and at times using more force than she wanted, the cracking and crunching sounds stopped in his neck.

She pushed on each side of his jaw and a couple of small pops came out. "Pull down on my jaw," the man asked his mouth only a bit more open than before.

"Are you sure? No I don't think I should," Lin once again worried. The only way she could do it would be to pry her fingers between his teeth and pull down. "I might pull out a tooth...or many."

"Oh, please you are doing so good! This is the last part. I promise! Money is no object...please."

And once again Lin was only concerned with the money. She put the tips of the fingers in his mouth and slowly started to pull down. There was a small sound and the jaw gave way a bit. She was able to get more of her fingers between the man's teeth and she pulled down. There was no give and she pulled with more might—POP!

Her hands came down in front of her stomach, but so did the man's lower jaw. There was a giant mouth in front of her. Her first thought was she had torn his jaw off, but what she saw was impossible. What was she seeing? She had no idea what was going on.

The man's eyes rolled back in his head and like the speed of a cobra his mouth came down over Lin's upper body. The mouth snapped shut with an iron grip. A muffled scream came from Lin.

The man stood up straight and tilted his head back, as he swallowed Lin much like a snake would swallow a mouse. In the seconds before the stomach acids started to burn and rot away her flesh, Lin didn't think about what her life could have been like in Hollywood. She didn't think about the loved ones she had left behind in China and the horrible life she had to lead during her brief time in America. In her last act in life, her hand tried to make it to her breasts so she could stop the money from falling out of her bra.

Story time at Jasmine Hills Home Living

Michael Miskelly sat at the table, a small trail of drool descending from the side of his mouth to the tip of his chin. It doesn't bother him; he doesn't even realize it's there. There is a sweet taste of apple in his mouth—he doesn't recall eating an apple or apple sauce, but the taste lingers. He looks down at the table in front of him and he sees a juice box, picks it up and has a sip. Apple juice–mystery solved.

There are voices around him, but he doesn't really pay attention. He sees there are three other men sitting down with him talking and laughing. They are sitting by a large window with a wonderful view of a garden and green lawn. There are old people outside some walking, many sitting in wheelchairs or on benches enjoying a beautiful day. Michael turns his head back to the table and takes another sip from the drink box. Apple juice nice.

It had been a year since he could remember the name of the building he lived in. Jasmine Hills Home Living–or in politically incorrect terms, an old folks home. He checked himself in seven-years ago. When he was able to communicate, he never mentioned family and kept to himself during most of the time. He was very polite with the staff and other residents, but never made any close friends and kept details of his former life to himself.

When the veil of dementia lowered itself over his memories the nursing staff thought it was important for him to socialize. The worst thing was to keep him isolated in his room, which would only worsen his mind and possibly his mood. The bright sitting room was an excellent area for him; lots of natural light and plenty of people to stimulate his senses.

The nurses asked the three men if it was okay to sit Mr. Miskelly at their table. They told them that he probably wouldn't say much, but it would be good for him to have some company. The three men happily agreed and added Michael's presence to their daily routine. They would wheel Mr. Miskelly to their table and the three men would sip on their coffee while Michael would sip on a drink box.

Occasionally Michael would say a few words, but most of the time it was incoherent or had nothing to do with what the men were talking about. That was okay, he seemed to be enjoying the daily routine and the men were pleased to have him.

Like many of their conversations the topics were related to the past. The topic today was an enjoyable discussion about the rebellious and trouble making side of them. Each man was asked what was the worst thing he had ever done. The first man admitted to cheating on his wife. The next man admitted to trying to once pick up a hooker that turned out to be an undercover officer. The man bumbled through his solicitation so badly the officer could tell this was his first time, and she let him off with a stern warning to never do it again. That one got a good laugh from the others. The last man in the group talked about how he stole a car and sold it for parts.

There was a lot of shocked faces and laughter around the table. The laughter subsided when the three men noticed laughing from the end of the table. It was Michael, looking down at his juice box, but wagging a finger at the three men. The three men laughed at the naughty-naughty gesture made by the finger.

A voice suddenly came out of Michael that they had not heard for a long time. "I... I remember", he softly spoke. The men were pleasantly surprised by Michael. Hopefully he was having a moment of clarity.

"What do you remember Mikey?" one of the men asked.

He kept looking at his juice box and reached a shaky hand out and took another sip. He was pleased to find out it was apple juice. He looked back up at the men and repeated "I remember."

The three men waited patiently for Michael to talk, they didn't want to rush him. But it was strange how he seemed to be sitting a little taller and his eyes seemed more aware. Probably just their imagination.

"I was married once."

They waited for more but all that happened was he took another, longer drink from his juice box. He put it down and asked for another.

One of the men quickly rushed to the nurse's station and got another drink box for him. They hoped he would be able to continue the conversation and not fall back into confusion.

With the drink box in front of him, Michael, with steady hands, removed the straw from the plastic and stabbed it down into the drink hole and took another deep sip. He looked back up and repeated, "I was married once." The men around the table smiled and were about to coax more out of him. But Michael did not need any coaxing. "I was married once, and I helped kill that bitch."

There was no haze in Michael's eyes. Whatever fog of confusion that had taken over during the last few years had been burned away, leaving the men staring in disbelief. Michael reached up and wiped the drool from the corner of his mouth and wiped it on his pants. He leaned in towards the men and told his story.

◊

Yep I was married once. I was young, dumb and full of cum. I made the mistake of marrying the first piece of tail I ever got. I didn't know better back then, hell many men make the same mistake. But I thought I was in love, and well I probably was in love for a while, but the feeling just kind of vanished. It wasn't even a slow decline. Suddenly one morning I woke up, and she was lying beside me, and I thought what the hell had I done?

I remember looking down at Kathy, that was her name, and thinking I don't love her anymore. I think the worst part was, I was bored with her. I was bored of fucking her, I was bored of talking to her, I was bored of my life. You would think a man in this situation would have left. Well, that was my second mistake with her. My first mistake was marrying her, and my second was not divorcing her right away.

How long did I wait in divorcing her you might be asking? Well, I lived with that bitch for another 12 years before she finally left me. To make things worse I had two kids with her—a boy and a girl. I swear she never cut the fucking umbilical cord with them. She fawned over those kids, hovering over them. They never left her side and they were weak minded because of it. I tried to toughen them up, but she always said I was being too hard on them.

Whatever. I would just drown out their annoying voices by drinking a few beers and watching whatever game was on TV. I would tell her to get my dinner and yell at her if she fucked up. The dumb cunt could never mash potatoes properly. I want my potatoes mashed properly, not all fucking lumpy and shit. I'd spit it in her face if it wasn't mashed properly or I would throw it at her.

She would leave the room crying like women fucking do. But she'd never slam the door. She learned that lesson. If she slammed the door, I would slam my fist into her. Women aren't all stupid let me tell ya. If you fucking smack them around enough, they learn. They learn.

By this point in our marital bliss we were living at the farm just outside Augerville, about 35 minutes from the coast. We grew corn that was my main crop. My daddy used to grow corn and his daddy used to grow corn. It was probably the one thing I was good at in life, besides fucking, of course. Yep, I had that farm running like a well-oiled machine. But that bitch of mine was jealous of it.

She was jealous of my skill and success at farming. She was jealous of my happiness there. I swear that dried up cunt was jealous of the corn. Often, she would drop hints of us moving into the city claiming it would be better for the kids and for us. Needless to say, after a few slaps those suggestions ended.

If I was to be honest with myself, I think I was too chicken to be the one that ended our marriage. I did everything in my power for her to be the one to end it. Well, it worked. One day in May she was just gone. I was working in the field and when I came in, she had packed her things and grabbed the kids and left.

That night I happily cooked my own dinner, watched a baseball game on TV and went to bed and had the best night's sleep in ages. I was alone with the corn and I loved it. I enjoyed being by myself and working around the farm. Sure, I missed having some cunt, but if I had an itch, I would just go into town and get a scratch.

My wife moved in with her sister Tammy. *Tammy the twat.* I hated that bitch. I knew she never liked me. I remember at my wedding she would smile towards me, but her eyes were cold. During my marriage to her sister she would barcly acknowledge me, speaking only to Kathy and the kids. If I had known she was going to be the one who'd send me to prison, I would have choked her to death the first time I met her.

During our separation I saw the kids every other weekend. Not that I really wanted them, but I figured it pissed Kathy off, so I took them in. They barely said anything to me. Maybe a "yes sir" or a "no sir". At the time I figured it was my bitch wife and her sister who were putting things into their heads to turn them against me.

They would just sit in their rooms reading books or go for walks in the cornfield. I think that is the only part of me that they shared. I loved walking in the corn, turning here and there. It didn't matter if I'd get turned around and lost. I knew I'd eventually find my way out and when I'd find my bearings I would go back in.

There is nothing greater on earth then feeling the corn leaf brush against me, its stalk reaching out above my head and hearing the wind blow through the field. Some listen to Beethoven or Mozart to relax–for me it is the wind through the corn field.

Life was blissful and quiet during the first few months away from my wife. Sometimes life throws you a curve ball, in my case, it was a woman with curves. She turned my quiet life into rocket ship fueled with chaos. And l loved every fucking moment of it.

Her name was Emma Saunders. Goddamn even saying that name after all these years gives me a chill down my spine and a tickle in my balls. She was responsible for turning my life upside down and inside out.

I met her at a strip club named Bonezy's. I was pent up and needed some release. I figured one of the whores in the club should be able to take care of it for me. I grabbed a beer and sat at the table off to the side. I nursed my beer and watched the girls. I was window shopping. I had the money and they had the honey.

When you wanted some release, you'd order a 'special dance' with one of the girls. To get this done you have to do business with the door man. The door man at Bonezy's was a stump named Ford. Ford was maybe about 5-foot-5 but he was as strong as a bull. I had worked with Ford as a kid, bailing hay at different farms through the county. As a boy, he was tiny, but god damn he was strong even then. He would outwork all of us other kids and even some of the adults.

I had seen one too many men, with a few too many drinks in them thinking they could get away with shit around Ford. When things got too rowdy, Ford would politely walk over to the person or persons and ask them to settle down or they would be asked to leave.

There was always one shit kicker who thought they weren't going to be told what to do by this little man. I have seen Ford slam men's heads into tables, guys knocked out with one punch and one memorable man who was, unfortunately for him, dragged out of the bar by his testicles.

I was always respectful to Ford and it didn't hurt that we had a history. I finished my beer and rose from my table ready to set up a 'special dance' though Ford when destiny interrupted. I can't remember the song, but I sure do remember when Emma stepped out onto that stage.

She had fiery red hair that curled down and rested on her elegant shoulders. Yeah, she had elegant fucking shoulders, that's the truth. Her face... her face was like an angel. I mean it was perfect. I didn't even notice her body because I was thunderstruck by her face. When I lowered my eyes, Jesus H. Christ, I had to fall back into my chair!

I just stared and was gobsmacked. My god, her tits and ass were perfect. That art fag Michael D'Angelo or whatever the fuck his name is, couldn't have created anything nearly this beautiful. When her set was over, she strutted off and I was sitting in my chair with an erection that could have knocked down a spruce tree.

I had to meet this piece of ass and I had to be cool. Offering money for a blow job or to fuck might not work with the woman, I didn't want to fuck things up. If she wasn't into selling herself, she might never speak to me again.

She must have had men hitting on her all the time, throwing out pathetic lines. I had to set myself apart from them, and not come on too strong. I didn't have any real game because I married young and just paid for sex. I took a deep breath and went to meet her.

Ford took me to the back where she was sitting in front of a mirror touching up her makeup. I casually walked up to her. I wasn't going to make eye contact with her because I was trying to play uninterested and casual. But when I saw her eyes, I couldn't take them away from hers. And the goddamndest thing was she locked eyes onto mine. We were both spellbound.

I fumbled out an introduction, not being cool at all, but managed to carry on. I told her that this was a small, boring town but I would love to take her out some time. I said that evening was no good because I had to wake up early for work. Through the week I was busy, but hopefully I could meet her next Saturday– no promises.

I said hopefully I could drop by after I've had dinner and cleaned up. I didn't give her a time or even ask if she was going to be here next Saturday. I just nodded a goodbye and said it was nice to meet her and managed to pull myself away from her eyes. My knees felt weak and my stomach was doing flips because I was so nervous. But I managed to walk away and somehow, I managed to make it through the week without rushing back to the club to see her.

Now I know I went there that night to have sex, but... this was different. There are a lot of strippers with the name Destiny, but she was my *destiny*. Somehow the stars aligned for us that night and I didn't want to fuck things up with a simple one-night stand.

My head was in the clouds. I day dreamed about the smell of her hair and the taste of her lips. I tell ya, it was as though I were a little boy with his first crush. I wasn't looking to fall in love, I just wanted someone to fuck. But... but, this girl had a spell on me and I was infatuated.

When I pulled into the parking lot at Bonzey's the following week, I forced myself to sit in the car and not rush in. I pulled into the lot at 9 and I think I must have sat in the car for an extra 20 minutes or so. I was trying to play it cool, but I was far from cool. My heart was pounding in my chest and my hands felt clammy. With weak knees, I made it inside, nodded my greetings to Ford and sat at the same table that I had a week ago. I'm usually a beer drinker, but I ordered a rye and ginger just to give my nerves an extra kick to settle down.

After a couple of drinks more and a handful of dancers later, Emma made her way onto stage. And by god, she was even lovelier than I remembered. I saw her looking around and she saw me and we instantly locked eyes again. Through her entire set she kept eye contact with me with a seductive grin on her face. I sat through her entire set with a hard-on again.

It was like I was a goddamned weak-kneed teenager again. That fucking woman had me in her power, and I was helpless to resist. At the end of her set she gestured for me with her finger to come over as she slipped behind the curtain. I again played it cool and sat at my table for a few minutes, mainly just to avoid showing the other perverts around me my cock that was trying to bust through my zipper.

When things settled down, I made my way to the back. She was near the back door and she smiled when she saw me. When I walked over to her she took me by the hand and took me outside. When the door shut behind us, she slammed me against the wall and started kissing me hard. Needless to fucking say, I was stunned, but I spun her around and pushed her hard against the wall. Harder then I intended— she gasped in surprise and then moaned a devilish little moan I could tell she loved it.

I know she loved it because she reached down and started undoing my belt. I reached under her short skirt and to my blessed surprise she was not wearing panties. She was wet and ready that little minx. I tell ya, when I entered her, I think I left my fucking body. I've had my share of pussy over the years, but goddamn, this was more than just sex. It was something that even after 40 plus years, I still can't explain our connection.

I like to pride myself on being able to hold my load when I'm fuckin' a chick, but she had me on the verge way too quick for my liking. She was gyrating against me and I told her to slow down. That seemed to excite her even more. She grabbed my ass and pulled me as tight to her as possible and she grinded into me with all her female wiles. I didn't stand a chance. I came so hard I thought I was going to pass out. I don't believe in soul mates or any of that other shit, but there was some kind of cosmic connection with Emma. We were destined to be with one another, our lives were meant to be together, our future linked. It was more linked then I think either one of us knew.

Anyways, Emma came home with me that night and she never left. We used to sit on the front porch at night smoking one of those "mar-idga-wanna" cigarettes and stare out at the corn. It was my first encounter with drugs. We fucked like rabbits and then smoke some of the devil's weed and drink. Goddamn that woman could drink! She could drink like a man and she wouldn't take any shit from one either.

I remember we got shit faced and got into an argument. I have no idea what it was about, doesn't even matter. During the argument I slapped her across the face. She turned around, not scared, not upset; she was fucking angry. She grabbed a beer bottle off the kitchen counter and smashed it off my head.

I dropped like a ton of bricks and she jumped on top of me and wrapped her hands around my throat. "Don't you ever pull that shit again or I will cut your dick off and feed it to the crows!" So, there I was, laying on the floor with my face turning red from being choked, blood running down the side of my head, smelling of old beer and I had the biggest hard on.

She could feel it, smiled and kissed me hard, but she kept her hands around my throat, easing up the choking only slightly. I rolled over on top of her and started to give it to her hard. My blood dripped onto her face and she moaned and rubbed it into her skin. I told her if she ever cut off my dick, I would slice her up and feed her to the hogs. She arched her back and came to my threat. She was a wild woman and I couldn't get enough of her.

Besides the weed and the constant sex, she introduced me to other drugs. A lot of pills. It was like flying without the wings. We used to pop a pill, see all kinds of colours and fucked like animals. I would hallucinate for hours at a time, colours melting in front of me. One time I saw dead relatives standing in the corner of the room watching me fuck. When it started to get scary, she would grab my head and tell me to look at her. She could always tell when I was on a bad trip, and I would just stare into her green eyes and get lost. It was those trips being lost in her beautiful eyes that I never wanted to wake up from. But I eventually did, and I couldn't wait to do it all over again.

Boy it was fun times. Yeah, the drugs probably sent us to our doom, but I think we would have eventually made it there anyway. There was chaos in our souls and neither of us knew how to fight it or wanted to fight it.

The kids still dropped by on the weekends and they wanted nothing to do with

Emma. That was fine with her because she rarely spoke to them and would usually work at the club during their visits. I knew the kids hated her and I hated them for it. Truth be told, I would pick her over them every time. I only took them because I know it bothered Kathy having another woman in the house, especially a stripper.

When Kathy picked them up, she would always be early, which was fine with me, and the kids would load in the car as soon as they could. We would talk for maybe a minute or two—it was always civil, but I could always see fear and mistrust of me in her eyes. And of course, she always brought that dirty cunt of a sister with her—safety in numbers I suppose.

Needless to say, Emma and I started going through a lot of money because of the drugs. I sold some old equipment that I kept for backup just in case my newer machines broke down. We also started to dip into me and Kathy's savings. At that point Kathy and I were still separated but she quickly went out and officially terminated our marriage with divorce papers. I knew it was a matter of time; so I wasn't surprised or angry. My new life had started, and I was glad to see my old one slipping away.

It was Emma that planted the poisoned seed in my head. She said with the divorce Kathy would want the farm and leave me/us with nothing. I never thought Kathy ever wanted the farm. It had been in my family and by what the kids had told me, they enjoyed where they were living. Emma kept picking at my doubts saying that Kathy wanted the farm only to sell it and keep the money for herself.

The doubt would scab over, and Emma would pick it off again putting fresh doubt in my mind. She reinforced her opinion that Kathy hated me, the kids hated me, and her cunty sister Tammy was probably filling Kathy's head full of vengeful ways to get back at me. Eventually Emma's words felt true. I was positive Tammy would love to see me down and out and taking my farm away from me was the easiest way for that to happen.

That night we tripped out on drugs and talked about killing Kathy. We talked for hours about how to do it and how we were going to get away with it. Our bedroom was a haze of smoke and empty beer and vodka bottles scattered around our bed.

We woke up around the same time the next day. Emma put a pot of coffee on while I just sat at the table looking outside the window, looking at *my* farm. She put the coffee in front of me and sat down with one of her own. She looked at me and asked, "Are we doing this?" I was still looking out the window and without hesitation I said, "Fuck yeah." When I looked over to her, Emma had a big grin on her face as she took a sip of her coffee.

On the day we decided to kill her, Kathy and Tammy dropped off the kids. I didn't want the kids around, so I let them go to their friend's house in town. I gave all the kids money, to see a double feature that was playing at the Regent Theatre that afternoon. As luck would have it, the parents of the other children asked if they could sleep over. I said sure they could, and that Kathy pick them up in the morning.

Now we didn't have to rush. Rushing causes mistakes and mistakes get you caught. Emma went to Bonzey's for a quick purchase from one of the girls and came back patting her purse saying we were good. We just sat back and waited.

We were ready. We had it planned; we even walked through it. The plan was to kill Kathy, but if her cunty sister was there, which was very likely, we had that planned out too. We pretended to tie the bitches up and timed ourselves driving from the farm to the ocean where we had a dump site, and even had a secondary site just in case there were people around. We had it planned! But we made the mistake of smoking a couple of joints to calm our nerves; and Emma without my knowledge, took a few pills and a couple of snorts of coke.

When Kathy and Tammy pulled up, unbeknownst the kids were at their friends for the night. I waited in the house and Emma hid in the barn. Kathy came to the front door while Tammy remained in the passenger seat. When I opened the door, I pulled a gun on Kathy and walked her back to the car. Tammy didn't even notice Emma sneak up and point a shotgun at her.

We tied both the bitches up and gave them each a hit of heroin, that Emma scored at Bonzie's. We didn't want them to overdose, so we gave them a small hit and after about 10 minutes we forced some downers in their mouth making them wash it down with some *Wild Turkey* bourbon. I took a lot of pleasure jamming that bottle into Kathy's mouth, pinching her nose and forcing her to swallow. I even poured some on her head–a farewell baptism.

Emma and I went back into the house and grabbed a couple of pillow cases to put on their heads for a drive to the coast. Both bitches had their hands tied behind their backs, so it was easy to slip on their hoods. I was about to put the pillow case over Tammy's head when I looked over and I saw Emma jam her pillowcase into Kathy's mouth. Emma started yelling at her, calling her every foul name in the book, saying that I was her man now. She spit in her face then pinched her nose closed. Kathy tried to struggle, but because of the drugs in her system she couldn't put up much of a fight.

I didn't put the pillow case on Tammy's head until she saw her sister's life end. We put them in the trunk of their car. I drove it; and Emma followed with our car. It was a little over a half an hour to the coast, and I was concerned Emma might get pulled over because she was drifting back and forth behind me. Fortunately for us there were no cops.

Everything was pretty much going as planned. I didn't expect Emma to kill Kathy, but that was fine. I should have killed Tammy though. If only I would have killed her in the driveway there would have been no arrest and I wouldn't have seen Tammy on the witness stand putting an end to Emma's and my love and freedom.

We came upon the bluffs and parked the cars. I dragged Tammy out and put her in the driver's seat and untied her hands. She was in no condition to run. If by chance she were to get behind the wheel of the car, she wouldn't be able to start it because I disconnected the spark plugs. I figured if the cops ever found the car and examined it, the disconnected spark plugs could have happened from the impact.

I just dumped Kathy in the back seat. It didn't matter as neither was wearing seatbelts so they could have been thrown around inside the car after the crash. When the police found the bodies, they will discover drugs and alcohol in their system. I planned on reporting her missing the following afternoon when she didn't pick up the children. Death by misadventure.

It was all going well until Emma fucked things up. I went back to my car, to check on something when I heard a gunshot. I turned around and I saw Emma sitting flat on her ass laughing. I ran over saw Tammy leaning over on the passenger side dead. Emma continued to laugh. I considered kicking her as hard as I could but the threat of the gun in her hands stopped me. I still remembered her threatening to cut off my prick; and with her impaired state, I could very much see her shooting me.

I screamed at her saying she ruined everything. It's really fucking tough to blame their deaths on a traffic accident when one of them has a bullet in the brain! I panicked and pushed the car that was in neutral over the edge of the cliff and into the ocean below. It was about a 30- or 40-foot drop. How that cunt survived, I have no idea.

I panicked and made some critical mistakes. The biggest one was checking to see if Tammy was actually dead. It never even occurred to me that I didn't see any blood splattered all over the place. When Emma shot, she was so fucked up, that she completely missed. In court Tammy said she felt the bullet pass just over her head, and it lodged into the roof of the car. She didn't mean to play dead, the gun shot scared her and made her fall onto the passenger seat. She admitted she probably would have sat back up, but the drugs had drained her energy, so she laid there, closed her eyes and waited for the next bullet which she was sure was coming.

After I pushed the car over, Emma and I got the fuck out of there. I planned on raking up the area clearing any foot prints and tire tracks. Well, it was all there a couple of days later for the police to match tire treads and foot prints.

Really, it just came down to bad luck. How that cunt survived was a miracle. A goddamn miracle. She broke her fucking pelvis, some ribs, her left ankle and one of her wrists—yet... yet, this fucking bitch managed to somehow get out and hold on to some fucking rock for nearly 12 hours until some fuck-head on a paddle board spotted her.

Emma and I were arrested and charged with murder and attempted murder. The police had Tammy's full statement, they found the pillowcases hidden in a barrel in the barn with hair samples on them. I should have burned the fucking thing, but I doubt it would have mattered. One of the girls at Bonzie's admitted to selling heroin to Emma shortly before the murder. There were the footprints and tire tracks at the dumping scene. Most damning was Emma admitting to it, saying it was me who killed Kathy.

I understand why she did it. She is a beautiful exotic bird that is not meant to be caged. She is a free spirit and prison would only kill her inside. She tried to plea, but it didn't matter. Tammy testified that is was Emma that killed Kathy and that she was the one who fired the gun. I didn't say a word to the cops or my lawyer. I knew we were done for.

I was right about Emma. I knew she couldn't handle prison. We were both given life sentences and three years into mine, one of the guards at the prison told me that... Emma hung herself in her jail cell. I couldn't imagine the horrors that led her to that choice. I don't want to think about her sobering up and guilt eating away at her or the prison rapes she endured. Not a single day has gone by without me dreaming of her. She was the love of my life; she was a star that burned too bright for this world. I like to think she hung herself because she couldn't stand the idea of never seeing me again. If I had the courage, I would have hung myself too, but I was too much of a coward.

I saw my children in court, and they could barely look at me. Years later they visited me for the first and only time. I guess they were in their late 20's, early 30's. I sat down behind the glass in the visitation room and they just stood on the other side. I could see the anger in their eyes. They never picked up the phone to talk to me, but I could read their lips and hear the muffled yelling. I could make out *bastard, murderer, prick, I hate you* and plenty of others. My daughter even spat on the glass.

No fucking class I tell ya! I just walked out of the room and never saw them again. I do keep in touch though. Through a lawyer, I make sure they are both sent a bottle of *Wild Turkey* on the anniversary of their mother's murder. The drink I baptized Kathy with before we killed her. Also, in my will I bequeath them both a case of *Wild Turkey*–they can have a toast to my memory.

I was released after 35 years in prison. I was a tough man to the women in my life, but in prison I found out I was weak. I did what I needed to do to survive and if that meant sucking a few dicks or taking it in the ass, so be it. At first, I tried to fight, but after numerous beatings I learned to just play the game. I'm not proud of it, but that's how it goes.

I never saw my farm again, but its memory kept me sane in prison. At night I would imagine walking between the rows of corn, smelling the clean air and getting down on my knees and running my fingers through the cool soil. My farm... someday I will... Emma...

◊

Michael looked around the room while the men sitting at the table with him stared in stunned silence. They had no idea a monster lived among them, hidden by dementia. Michael looked at the drink box in front of him and slowly raised it to his mouth, "Mmm, apple juice," he said to himself.

A small trail of juice ran down from his lip making its way to his chin where it slowed down and faded away. Michael Miskelly sank back into his wheel chair and any hint of lucidity in his eyes disappeared; his story was over–he didn't even know he told it. He turned his head to the side and focused his attention on a plant in the corner of the room. He looked at the plant and smiled. He loved the shape of its leaves.

The Vacation

Michael stood on the stage and he was bombing. It was amateur night at the comedy club and this was one of the things he had planned for his vacation. Like with most of the other aspiring comedians, the crowd would chuckle occasionally with the loudest laughs coming from friends and family that were brought along for support. Booing and heckling newcomers was frowned upon.

"I was watching my dog the other day. I was wondering what it was like to be a dog, so I tried something new. I peed with my leg cocked up. It didn't work too well —I just ended up peeing on my leg and getting my sock wet."

There were some forced smiles and a couple of people chuckled out of politeness and nothing more. "Pppppppppfffffffffffffttttttttttttttt" from the back of the room from a man who acted as if he just got the joke. He started laughing loud and long.

Michael knew the man was laughing at him bombing and not at his joke. He had a very bad feeling as soon as he saw the man enter the club a few minutes earlier. Others in the crowd stared at the man, many thinking he was rude to make fun of a person trying comedy for the first time. "This is not going to end well," thought Michael. But like a pro, Michael carried on.

"I was pretty upset at the time, so I rubbed my nose in it. And you know what? It worked, I never did it again. Now I have to learn not to drag my butt across the carpet."

This time he got a better laugh, but he was hoping for more. This was one of his best jokes. Again, the man in the back of the club started roaring with fake laughter. Michael could see the man pretending to wipe tears away from his eyes. Michael watched his heckler waiting for him to stop. The two men locked eyes–things definitely weren't going to end well.

The couples that were seated closest to the laughing man started shifting their chairs away from him. They weren't aware they were doing it, but something deep down in them knew it was not safe being near him.

"I had to give up being a dog completely when I started sniffing people's crotches when I first met them." It was a bit tasteless of joke for Michael, and it had been done before by 10-year-olds across the planet, but considering it was his first time on stage, he didn't have anything better.

The man in the back roared out laughing but it was not a human noise. It sounded like many animals crying out in pain. The people in the audience became suddenly aware that they were in the middle of a horror movie and not a comedy club. They jumped out of their chairs and screamed in panic. Blood started pouring from the man's eyes and mouth as he continued making a gurgling screaming sound.

"Not now you... dick," Michael said. His first attempt at stand-up was now ruined—well, more ruined. He thought he had a great closer about using the showers at a gym, but now he would never know if it would have gone over. Michael just gripped the microphone stand tightly as the bleeding man stood up from his chair.

The man started to grow as the cloths came tearing off his body. His head split open to show a demon face with red scaly skin and horns on top of his head. The body continued to grow until it towered over 10 feet. All the audience members and staff were running for the doors in complete panic. Michael just stared at the demon.

Michael picked up the microphone stand and threw it at the demon. It had no time to react as it impaled his head and was driven back and pinned it to the wall. Michael walked up to the demon. The skin was turning to ash, but a smile was still on the demon's face.

"Thanks for ruining my night," he said as he flicked the demon with his finger. The body disintegrated into a pile of ash and disappeared.

It was a crappy start to archangel Michael's vacation.

◊

When he left the comedy club Michael could hear the police sirens approaching. There would be no reports of a demon in the club. All the people would claim there was a crazy man with a gun and when the police inspected the club there would be no ashes left from the demon. The mic-stand in the wall would be a head scratcher with nobody having any idea how it ended up embedded in the wall. When demons and angels fight around humans, their minds are erased of what happens – God and Satan agreed about playing behind the scene roles in the lives of humans. It would be too much for the Human psyche.

Michael looked around the city wondering what to do next. He didn't want to be here, but he didn't have a choice.

◊

"Michael," God called out. "Can you come over here for a moment please?" The archangel was talking to a couple of angels about the day's agenda when he was called. He let out a sigh because he knew it would be about his vacation time. He had been brushing it off for a while but found it harder and harder to get out of it.

The two angels that were with him gave him a grin. "What are you two grinning about?" he snarled.

Michael walked over to God. To every angel and inhabitant of Heaven, God appeared to them in whatever image they had of God. To some God appeared to as a ball of light, to Michael, God first was just a voice with no figure, but now always appeared as a little girl.

"Michael, why are you avoiding your vacation?" she asked.

"I'm really busy around here. I must make sure our Angels are ready for battle if they come face to face with any demons. We always have hot spots popping up all over the place that we contain..."

"Michael please sit."

Michael sat down on the bench that appeared behind them and when he sat down, they were transported to Michael's favorite spot. It was a green grass inlet surrounded by waterfalls. Some were towering with a powerful flow, while some were broken up by rocks making it to the bottom in a mere trickle. Each was gorgeous and had a hypnotic quality to them. Michael would spend quiet moments here watching the water cascading down and churning in the water below. A soft, refreshing mist would sometimes blow in and the smell of the water was pure. It was all perfect.

"This isn't fair God," Michael said to the girl who had a small smile on her face.

"When was your last vacation Michael?"

"I don't need a..." he started to plead again.

"Michael, I need you to take a vacation," God said. "I know you are busy. You do a fantastic job and you are my most trusted angel. You are a champion for humanity and a champion for Heaven."

"But?" Michael asked with a smile.

"But... If you are going to save human lives, to free their spirit and protect them, you need to understand them. You need to experience the human condition Michael. You need to know why they sin. You need to know why they love. You need to know what makes them human."

God looked around at the waterfalls and curled her toes through the green grass. "You love this place," not asking a question.

"It's perfect."

God smiled again. "Well humans are not Michael. Regardless of how kind and caring a human being is, they are never and will never be perfect.

"Sending you down to Earth is a chance for you to learn. You'll be free to do whatever you choose down there. I won't be watching, and I'll never know. I just want you to experience humanity.

"If you are to understand sin, you will have to experience sin. I'm not saying go down there and kill somebody but understand the souls we are trying to guide. You will never understand humans until you have experienced the human condition."

God was right—of course. Reluctantly he agreed that after he wrapped up some loose ends he would go on vacation. "You're going now Michael," God said while appearing to be distracted by one waterfall. Michael groaned and gave in. He wasn't getting out of this "Fine! I'm going but I'm not going to like it!" he said. Just before he flashed away to Earth, he saw God laugh and smile. Michael's felt a wave of love when he saw her smile.

◊

As he walked down the street, he saw a lot of lost souls. People who were looking for and questioning their faith. People who had given up on themselves or the people around them. People who saw only money and missed all the beautiful things around them. Michael was on vacation, it was not his job to help these people, there were other angels sent down to deal with that. Michael was here to be one of them.

One of the most popular spots for angels on vacation is the bar. They see so many people dealing with alcohol that many want to experience it for themselves. Michael was staying clear of the bars.

So many angels in previous years have gotten so drunk they spent most of their holidays vomiting and being hung over. One year, an angel stumbled out of a bar in a blind stagger and was hit and killed by a bus.

Angels can't die on Earth. He went right back up to Heaven. The rest of the angels laughed at him and teased him. There is a lot of joking, pranks and having fun in Heaven. It is not all serious like some religions would like you to believe.

Michael took a deep breath—he was off to experience pleasure of the flesh.

◊

He kept to the seedy side of town. Not because that was where the sinners were, he could have gone to the rich side of town and seen as much sin. He stayed in the seedy side to pick up a prostitute, because they were easier to spot and more available. He was on earth for a short period of time, and this was the quickest way to pick up a woman.

He stopped in front of a woman with short shorts and a tight t-shirt, fishnet stockings and high-heeled boots. If there were a hooker Halloween costume, it would be this getup. "Looking for a good time hon?" He has found his prostitute.

"Yes I am," he replied simply enough.

"You a cop? You have to tell me if you are a cop."

"Me? No, I'm not a cop."

She looked him up and down. Nicely dressed, looked clean, hopefully a guy with cash–he was worth the risk. "What's your name hon?

"Michael".

"Well Mikey, what are you looking for?"

Michael just shrugged not really sure what to say. "I'm just looking for a good time, that's all."

"That's all, huh?" she said taking a final drag from her cigarette. "Okay Mikey, we can have a good time, sure."

"What's your name," Michael asked innocently enough.

The whore snorted out some laughter, "My name is Sugar, Mikey. That is because I taste *so* sweet." She accented that with a lick of her lips. "You want to go across the street?" She nodded to a cheap hotel she takes most of her Johns to.

"Well, I have a room about 15 minutes from here. I would rather just walk there. If you wouldn't mind."

She wasn't planning on wasting her time walking with a guy for 15 minutes and then just getting stiffed out of money. Some of these losers were lonely men who just wanted a woman to talk to instead of fucking. Mikey could be one of these guys. Her time was money.

"I need some money up front Mikey, give me some cash and we can walk to where ever you want... within reason."

Michael reached into his back pocket and fished out his wallet. One benefit of being an angel on vacation was the ability to call upon whatever he needed. His wallet would always have as much money as necessary.

But the question was how much money to take out? How much did a prostitute cost? He looked up at Sugar and back down to his wallet. He didn't want to hurt her feelings by offering a small amount. He took out some bills and counted them quickly. He then looked up at Sugar who was closely watching him.

"Is $950 good enough for... a down payment?" he asked unsure of how to put it any other way.

Sugar nearly choked on her gum. $950, up front? The most she had ever made off of one guy was $350 and part of that money was stealing it from his wallet when he went to the washroom. She asked to see one of the hundreds, and Michael passed it over with no questions asked.

She had seen plenty of fake bills in her time. She had guys trying to rip her off all the time, and she in turn had used fake bills to rip off others. She held it up to the streetlight, turning it repeatedly, and felt the bill by rubbing it between her thumb and forefinger.

The fucking bill was real! This guy was just some rich asshole, who just wanted to go slumming for a night. Well, she was game.

"Okay Mikey," she said snatching the bills from his hand. "Let's go! And if you want, I can stop off somewhere and pick up some blow for us. We can do some lines, or shoot up, whatever the fuck you want to do. We can get sky high and I'll let you fuck me all night long."

Michael winced at the bad language but told her he just wanted to... fuck. It felt foreign coming from his lips, but it was a first for him–swearing. It didn't make him feel any different, but he did feel it made him sound less intelligent.

His hotel was a few blocks away. It was cheap but he didn't need much. He only went there to sleep, which was a strange experience in itself. Sugar looked up at the hotel and moaned. She was hoping he was going to call a cab or a limo. This dude had so much cash on him, why was he staying at this shit heap? She got scared and wondered what the deal was with this guy. She only briefly considered saying no, but the idea of losing the cash and she need to score some heroin. The temptation was too over powering.

When they got up to the room Sugar ran in and jumped out flat on the bed giving out a girlish scream. "Got anything to drink Mikey?"

"Ummm," Michael said looking sheepishly around the room. "What would you like?"

"I seriously doubt you have brandy, so I'll take whatever you got."

Michael walked over to the dresser opened the top drawer and pulled out a bottle of brandy and a snifter–again summoning whatever he needed.

"I hope this is good enough?" he said bringing the bottle over to her.

"Huh. You usually keep booze and glasses in your top drawer?"

Michael couldn't think of an excuse, so he just shrugged.

"Holy shit!" Sugar gasped as she bolted up in the bed holding the bottle. "How old is this! This must cost a fortune!" The label was in some language she couldn't understand, and the cork had a wax seal around it. She examined the bottle holding it up the light seeing the beautiful golden-brown inside. This couldn't be legit.

She was going to ask if he were sure, but hell, when would she ever get this opportunity again. Besides, he did offer. From her purse she pulled out a knife she carried just in case any assholes got out of line. She never considered it might frighten her john, and Michael never reacted to it. Honey cut off the wax and opened the bottle and quickly poured some into the glass. She was afraid she was going to spill it, with her hands slightly shaking in excitement.

She gave a sniff and moaned in pleasure to the most incredible smell she had ever encountered. A wave of sweet memories swept over her. He grandfather was a brandy connoisseur. Brandy was his passion, but he wasn't an alcoholic like many she met later in life.

When she was young, he would always show her how to swirl the brandy in the snifter. To put one's nose in the glass and breath out gently. First you tasted with your nose by giving short sniffs then taking a sip and swirl the drink in your mouth, exploring the flavors.

Of course, she was only allowed to sniff and when she turned 17 her grandfather would let her sip but kept an empty glass nearby to spit it out. She sometimes swallowed a sip and her grandfather would pretend to be upset, but he was very loving and the only person in the family who she related to and who understood her. He passed away when she turned 18. She was devastated by the loss and started her self-loathing downward spiral.

As a little girl she always had a kinship with her grandfather. He had the patience to listen to her as she would babble about whatever four or five-year-old had on their mind. He always had a smell of Old Spice and would tickle her neck with his beard. He had the worst jokes and he made her laugh every time.

During her high school years, she would spend more time with him than her friends. Her parents thought it odd and encouraged her to spend more time socializing with people her own age, but his face lit up every time he saw her, and she was always excited to visit.

When he died suddenly of a heart attack she was devastated. The tears flowed for weeks and her parents made the unfortunate mistake of saying she had to get over it. She screamed at them and they wished they could take it back, knowing they sounded callous.

She started drinking to ease her grieving and that started more intense arguments with her parents. They said she can't turn to alcohol to numb her pain, suggesting she should see a psychiatrist or psychologist for help.

Oversensitively she took that as meaning they thought she was crazy and unstable.

As a punishment towards them she started drinking more and using drugs. As the drinking became more often and the drugs stronger, the fights became bigger until the day she decided to run away. It had been four years since she last saw her parents–what seemed like a lifetime ago.

She gave a small sip and it went down smoother than she hoped. She wanted to gulp it down before Mikey took the bottle away wanting to fuck her, but when she looked around the room, she saw him sitting quietly in a chair by the window.

She savored every swallow, convinced she would never have a moment like this again, knowing any drink after this would taste tainted to her pallet.

She drank another two glasses and looked over a Mikey. She put the glass and bottle on the nightstand, pulled off her top and slowly removed her shorts. She slowly removed her bra running her fingers slowly over her hardening nipples. She got a shiver of delight. It was really good brandy! She slightly lifted her butt and removed her panties.

Michael watched from across the room not knowing what to say or what he should do.

She rubbed her fingers over her vagina and moaned loud enough for Mikey to hear her. She spread her legs wide and in a sexy voice said, "come over and get it Mikey, you deserve it!"

During their sexual encounter Sugar was thrusting underneath him, digging her nails into his back. Michael on the other hand, while enjoying the sensation, particularly liked the closeness. He loved her being in his arms and the closeness to her. He got an understanding to the appeal of sex and the intimacy of it.

During the *act* he took a moment and explored her mind and memories. He knew he was on holiday, but it was tough to turn off the angel switch.

He saw the happiness in her life then her grandfather's passing. He saw the pain in her parent's eyes. He saw 'Sugar' turn to drugs and alcohol to take away the pain. Her parents tried everything they could do to rescue their daughter, but the clutches of addiction were too strong.

Using tough love, they told their daughter it was either her family or the drugs. Sugar had chosen heroin or perhaps it had chosen her. She ran way and found the lights of the big city. Plenty of men had the drugs she wanted if she gave them what they wanted.

She ended up with a pimp who put an end to Johns beating her, robbing her and holding a knife to her throat. But in return he shared her with his friends, but as long as heroin ran in her veins, she just closed her eyes and tried to distance her mind from her body.

She had not seen or heard from her family in a few years, not knowing if they were alive or dead. She did not know if she would be alive from month to month, just waiting for an overdose of cocaine or heroin to finish her off. A long time ago Tammy, the name she had in a previous life, died and now 'Sugar' was sure to follow.

Sugar could not see the tears in Michael's eyes. When the *session* was over, she sat on the edge of the bed dressing, already anticipating a score. "Damn it Mikey, you're a good fuck. I shit you not."

Michael reached over and softly grabbed her arm where the needles marks traced down her arm, with some collapsed veins under the skin. She looked down at her arm. She didn't want anyone to look or touch those horrible scars, but she was silent, and let him continue.

He slowly traced the scabs from old needles and new tracks with the tip of his finger. The marks faded away and new fresh skin appeared. Damage veins were healed and the body's need for heroin, cocaine and alcohol were gone. Any viruses were vanished, and any ailments were cured. At that moment, Sugar was the healthiest person on the planet.

She got up from the bed with tears running down her eyes, but they were not tears of pain and anger any more. She quietly dressed and walked across the room and opened the door ready to leave, a healthy glow to her skin and life back in her eyes. She looked back to the bed.

"Maybe it's time you went back home Tammy," said the archangel.

She tilted her head at him, realizing she never gave him her proper name. "Yeah," she said. "I think it is. Thank you... Michael."

He lay back in bed when she shut the door and he fluffed the pillow. He closed his eyes and waited for the strange sensation of sleep to take over. He had a small smile on his lips. He may have been on vacation, but sometimes everyone needs an angel's help.

◊

The next morning, he figured he would spend a few more days on Earth. He had work to do back in Heaven, and he already had an eventful vacation.

He toured the city looking at the people and their actions and reactions to life. They were all in such a hurry and for what? So many missed the simple day-to-day pleasures; he felt sad for many of them. Michael felt more pity on many of the men in their power business suits, than he did for the homeless. Many of the homeless were aware of the things they had lost, the men in the business suits had no idea.

He was walking towards the theatre district when he suddenly sensed evil. He turned left down the next street and turned right into a small alleyway. Walking towards him were two men. He knew one of them well.

"Oscar," said Michael to small man wearing a torn jean jacket with a peace symbol on the left breast. "What brings you out here?

"Michael," he silently mouthed to himself and stopped.

The bigger man beside him, muscle bound and dressed in slacks and a sports coat said, "Fuck off you. Oscar how does this guy know you?"

"He is an angel."

The bigger man's eyes turned blood red and razor teeth made an evil smile on his face. He took a step forward but Oscar but an arm across him, halting him in his tracks.

"He is an angel, archangel Michael." And with that the evil grin turned into a worried frown.

"Who is your big friend there Oscar?"

"I'm..."

Michael cut him off. "I wasn't talking to you was I now?"

"Ahh, this is just a new guy. Just showing him about that's all."

"Aww, that's nice! Just a couple of demons taking a nice stroll huh?"

"Come on, we can do it. It's two against one!" said the large demon.

"Lenny shut up!"

"Yeah Oscar! Lenny is right, you have me out numbered," said Michael with a grin.

Oscar put up a finger to Michael as if he could take a moment. Michael nodded in the affirmative. Oscar pulled on Lenny's sleeve and turned their back. "Listen to me! Shut up. WE cannot win in a fight. He is an archangel. If we had 10 or 20 more, I still wouldn't like our chances. He is Heaven's most powerful angel. You don't stand by my side and try to pick a fight with an archangel. Got it?"

"Sure but,"

"No buts. You got me?" he said firmly.

"Yes".

"Sorry Michael" Oscar started to say.

"Sorry! Sorry! You're apologizing to him! Stop acting like a..."

Michael reached into his back pocket and pulled out a small white object that looked like a toothpick, which glowed bright. Oscar sidestepped away from Lenny. Michael threw the object at Lenny, which grew to the size of a spear and pierced the demon's chest. Light poured out his eyes, nose and mouth then he exploded in a blazing white fireball.

Oscar looked at where Lenny once stood and then at archangel Michael.

"You wanna go for a beer?"

"Absolutely," Michael said.

-

"So, what are you doing down here Michael?"

"Vacation." Michael said taking a sip of his beer not caring much for the taste.

"Do anything exciting?"

"No but I might go to an amusement park tomorrow and see what that is all about."

"An amusement park? God gives you a vacation and you want to experience the human feeling of eating too much cotton candy and corn dogs while you throw up after riding on one too many roller coasters. What a waste."

The demon and angel had known each other for millenniums. Once upon a time they were angels in Heaven, until there was a separation between Lucifer and God. Angels took sides, and Oscar chose Lucifer's side. Despite the many times they were at odds for human souls, they would still sometimes take time to catch up and sometimes talk of the old days.

"What were you two doing down here?" Michael asked. "I know you two weren't just going for a walk in the city. You only gather when something big is going to go down."

Oscar shrugged. "We felt something. I'm not sure what, or if it is going to happen. It felt pretty violent, and when we saw you, I thought for sure something was going on. I thought you were going to stop us before it even happened. I don't feel too much of it right now, so instead of a mass killing maybe someone thought better of it and just went home to cool off.

"By the way," asked Oscar. "Where you around a comedy club the other night?"

Michael cringed inside and he knew he was busted. There was no point in denying it. "I was on stage."

The demon slapped his knee and let out a genuine laugh. "I knew it! I didn't know it was you, but that explains it! Dezmond came back to Hell and said he met an angel in a comedy club. He never said who he ran into and he admitted he knew he had no chance of winning the fight, but he couldn't pass on the chance. He wouldn't tell us, he said we had to guess."

"Were you any good?"

Michael moved his hand in a so-so manner.

Oscar looked at Michael and laughed. "What?"

"You know for God's mightiest angel you are pathetic. A comedy club? Now an amusement park? You're better than that.

"You know what you have to do?" said Oscar taking a sip of his beer and pushing it aside. Obviously, he didn't care much for the taste of beer either. "Let me ask you something Michael, have you ever killed a man?"

"Oscar I'm an angel. I'm not going to kill anybody."

"You're on vacation. God isn't looking and he won't know."

"I'm not going to kill anyone."

"Just hear me out Michael. You want to experience what it is like to be human? Humans are violent. They start wars, they kill for passion and kill because someone cut them off in traffic. They beat their spouses and their children and go to *your* churches to ask forgiveness only to start it all over the next day.

"They talked about all the inhuman suffering which had touched the world in recent history. Adolph Hitler against Jews, Harry Truman dropping two atomic bombs, Joseph Stalin and Pol Pot killing their own people. They may have become industrial and feel a sense of accomplishment with their technology, but they haven't learned how to stop killing each other.

"How can you save their souls if you really don't know the shadow of darkness that sometimes covers it? You are the most powerful angel in Heaven, yet you are its biggest hypocrite because you refuse to see or experience a side of them which they say is human nature."

Oscar tossed some money on the table and started to rise. "Have a fun time on the *Screamer* at the amusement park my old friend. I'm sure that is why God sent you down to experience human feelings and life–to wait in line to get on rides."

◊

Michael wandered the city walking in the general direction of his hotel. He didn't want to be on vacation, he never wanted to leave

Heaven. God knew that. This was a waste of time; he had more important things to do.

Across the alley that he was wandering, a man approached out of the dark. His stride was determined, his head was lowered, but his eyes up were and focused. Like he had done many times, the knife came out of his pocket in a flash.

"Give me your wallet mother-fucker!" The angel looked at the man with shock.

"Um, what?" Michael said not knowing what the man was angry about.

"Give me your money or I will cut you, bitch!"

Michael reached in his back pocket. "Umm, do you want a certain amount? Not sure what I have, just wait..."

The blade swished through the air catching Michael at the ear lobe and sliced deep down the side of his face. He could feel the knife against his teeth as it sliced against bone. Blood poured down his face and he turned and lowered his head and opened his eyes to see a shocking amount of blood pouring onto the dirty concrete.

"If you make one move, I will plunge this into your chest." The young man picked up the wallet Michael didn't even know he had dropped. "I cut you, because you be stupid!

Don't be anymore stupid." Michael slowly tilted his head up and his eye met with his attacker.

In a flash the attacker was pinned against the brick wall and Michael had his hand clasped over the young man's hand that held the knife. The attacker who stood well over six feet tall looked down at the man that had him pinned him against the wall. He thought with the height advantage, the element of surprise and a weapon this would be an easy robbery, but the smaller man was incredibly strong.

The man shot a knee into Michael's crotch, followed with a punch from his free hand. It was like hitting a marble statue. His knee and fist flared in pain. The bloody man's other hand that was down by his side was now pressed against his forehead. There was so much pressure he thought for sure his eyes were going to pop out of their sockets.

When he cut the man, he figured it was a done deal. He'd grab the wallet, take whatever jewelry the guy had and leave. Having a huge gash across the face, the guy should be focused on not dying. The last thing he expected was for him to fight back.

Michael, with his attacker pinned against the wall, didn't expect to be harmed and he didn't expect his power come rushing in. It was an automatic reaction. Now a new feeling came forward during his eventful vacation–anger. Most of the day he felt pity for humanity, but looking into his attackers' eyes, the archangel just felt fury.

"Jason why would you do this?" the young man's eye grew. He didn't know this man. "Are you a servant of the Devil, Jason? I know you don't believe in God. I know you have killed in the past. Drive by shootings and stabbings. You even killed an old woman when you were just a young boy stealing her pocket book. Did you know that Jason? You snatched her purse and ran away. But while you fled, she fell to the ground and died of a heart attack."

Jason found himself staring into the eyes of his victim. He couldn't help but whimper out in pain from thc man's grip. His hand was still wrapped the knife, but the strong man squeezed it tight making it impossible to let go. A sudden recognition made his stomach turn, the gash on the side of the man's face was totally gone. Impossibly gone.

The incredibly strong man moved Jason's hand with the knife in it and brought the edge of the blade under the frighten man's chin and pressed it slightly into the skin.

"I know you don't believe in Heaven Jason, but do you believe in Hell? Do you think if you cause enough anarchy on earth the Devil will praise you and make you a minion?"

"What are you talking about man?" Tears ran down Jason's eyes as the knife went a bit deeper. The man was mad, rambling about God and the Devil. He knew he was going to die–the dude was some religious nut with retard strength. He never thought he was afraid of death, but at this moment terror spread across his body

"Do you know why the Devil was thrown out of Heaven, Jason? He was an angel and his name was once Lucifer. Well, Lucifer was angered by human weakness. He got tired of the all killing, robbing and maiming. He wanted those humans to suffer and feel pain, even more intense than what they inflicted. Are you following me so far Jason?"

Michael slowly twisted the knife and sank it slightly more into the man's flesh, trickles of blood ran down the blade.

"God believes in forgiveness. He can send a man or woman back to earth–reincarnation if you like and have them experience the same pain that they inflicted.

"Well Lucifer didn't like that. He said it was a vicious circle. God tried to tell him to give humanity time. By learning and experiencing life, eventually humanity will find their way.

"Well I don't need to tell you the rest. Lucifer and some other angels that agreed with him formed Hell."

The knife moved sideways under Jason's chin slightly and worked its way deeper into him.

"Some people think that by killing for and worshipping Lucifer that they will sit by his side in Hell." Michael lowered his lips to Jason's ear and whispered. "Let me tell you the obvious Jason the Devil hates you! All that awaits you is pain!

"Demon's and angels have fought countless times for souls. But it is only for the souls of doers of evil deeds. Lucifer has used innocent souls to hurt evildoers by possession, but when the innocent dies, he will leave their side and allow them to enter Heaven's Gate."

"Leave me alone man! You crazy man! You crazy!"

Michael carried on.

"But you, you my friend are marked." Michael looked all over the attacker's face. "I can see the mark on you, and I can smell it on you. You are marked for Hell, and I'm not sure there is a damn thing you can do about it now.

You can try to lead the righteous life and do good–but the evil you have done, well it may be too late."

"Please!" Jason said sobbing praying this crazy man would let him go.

"With your mark," Michael said slicing the blade up towards his chin. The blood was a steady stream down Jason's neck and covering Michael's hand. "Demons are watching you. They are close to you, ready for you to die. They will try to pounce on your soul before *we* have a chance to save you.

"Satan wants you to experience more pain and suffering then you can ever imagine. All because you want to be a tough guy. You want to make money the easy way instead of working for it. You find it easier to hate then to love. You ignore the world around you and focus only on your own wants. Well, just remember Jason, Hell wants you!

"And they will torture your soul physically and mentally. I'm not talking about this flimsy excuse," Michael said referring to the human body that he added more pressure to and Jason screamed out in more pain. "Satan himself will torture your soul to its absolute breaking point and let me assure you Jason, the souls breaking point is well past anything you can imagine."

Michael could hear the bones in Jason's hand breaking. "Satan has never released a soul he has taken, and we have yet to free one. Our armies have attacked Hell on three occasions, and we have yet to reach any tortured souls." Unlike battles on Earth when killed angels and demons die they return weakened to Heaven and Hell–when they are killed in battle in Heaven or Hell, they do not rise again. "I will fight for your soul Jason and you better pray I am there to greet you when you die!"

He let go of the man and threw the knife to the side. Jason lay on the ground in pain and fear. This motherfucker was crazy–it was safer to just not move. Michael turned around and threw up in a garbage can. He raised his head as tears ran down his cheeks. He never wanted to experience anger and violence against humanity ever again.

There was a chance that he saved the man's soul by scaring him. He would have to totally change his life and become a righteous man–or it might be too late, Lucifer might have his eyes set on him. In time Jason may just believe that Michael was a bible thumper, high on PCP with drug induced strength and religious obsession.

His vacation was now over. There would be no amusement park, no more prostitutes, and no more stand-up comedy. He had a war to prepare for. There were no current plans to attack Hell, but Satan and his hoard had grown in strength–possibly more than the angels wanted to admit. He had to go back home to prepare, but first he would go to the waterfalls and reflect on his time on Earth. He had learned more than he expected.

One thing he would do would be to keep a close eye on his attacker, Jason. There were many eyes on Jason. His eternal soul depended on who reached him first.

Acknowledgements

Thank you to my editor John Ross for his help and encouragement with this project. I cannot thank you enough. Any mistakes in this book are property of the author alone. Thank you to Jenny Groat who again did a wonderful job on the cover, it turned out terrific. Thank you to Paul Gibson who saved me by doing the book layout and an awesome job on the back cover. You're a lifesaver. A thank you to my sister-in-law Cheryl Pratt. During the 'life is stranger than fiction' days of Covid-19 she is a nurse at North York General Hospital in Toronto, doing a job I could never do—you rock! As always, thank you to my wife Christine each and every day. You are my rock and my best friend, thank you for putting up with me and not smothering me in my sleep—I love you. To my wonderful son Ryan—watching you grow up has been one of the biggest joys in my life! You are an inspiration and you are my hero! And to you the reader, thank you for taking a chance on a self-published author.

About the author

Glenn Lomas lives in Newcastle, Ontario with his wife Christine, son Ryan and their little brown dog Loki. This is the author's second book.

www.ingramcontent.com/pod-product-compliance
Lightning Source LLC
Chambersburg PA
CBHW072234190626
46809CB00018B/2062